PENGUIN CRIME FICTION

RUMPOLE'S RETURN

John Mortimer is a playwright, a novelist, and a lawyer. During World War II he worked with the British Crown Film Unit and published a number of novels before turning to the theatre. His plays include *The Dock Brief*, *What Shall We Tell Caroline?*, *The Wrong Side of the Park*, and *Voyage Round My Father*. His translations of Feydeau have been performed at the National Theatre in London, and he recently completed six plays for television on the life of Shakespeare. He has written many film scripts and television and radio plays. His novels *Rumpole of the Bailey* and *The Trials of Rumpole*, which first introduced Horace Rumpole, have also been made into television series and are published by Penguin Books. John Mortimer lives with his wife and young daughter in the Chilterns, England.

John Mortimer

Rumpole's Return

Penguin Books

Penguin Books Ltd, Harmondsworth,
Middlesex, England
Penguin Books, 625 Madison Avenue,
New York, New York 10022, U.S.A.
Penguin Books Australia Ltd, Ringwood,
Victoria, Australia
Penguin Books Canada Limited, 2801 John Street,
Markham, Ontario, Canada L3R 1B4
Penguin Books (N.Z.) Ltd, 182–190 Wairau Road,
Auckland 10, New Zealand

First published in Great Britain by
Penguin Books 1980
Reprinted 1981
First published in the United States of America by
Penguin Books 1982

Copyright © John Mortimer, 1980
All rights reserved

Printed in the United States of America by
George Banta Co., Inc., Harrisonburg, Virginia
Set in Linotype Plantin

Except in the United States of America,
this book is sold subject to the condition
that it shall not, by way of trade or otherwise,
be lent, re-sold, hired out, or otherwise circulated
without the publisher's prior consent in any form of
binding or cover other than that in which it is
published and without a similar condition
including this condition being imposed
on the subsequent purchaser

For Penny

Else I my state should much mistake
    To harbour a divided thought
From all my kind – that, for my sake,
    There should a miracle be wrought.

No, I do know that I was born
    To age, misfortune, sickness, grief:
But I will bear these with that scorn
    As shall not need thy false relief.

Nor for my peace will I go far,
    As wanderers do, that still do roam;
But make my strengths, such as they are,
    Here in my bosom, and at home.

Ben Jonson: 'A Farewell to the World'

Chapter One

One dark, wet and almost arctic night in springtime (in fact it was Thursday, 13 March, and the sort of brutal English weather which ought to have made me profoundly grateful for where I was at the time) a 35-year-old clerk in the Inland Revenue named Percival Simpson left his evening class in Notting Hill Gate and went, as he always did on Thursday nights, into the Delectable Drumstick to buy his take-away supper. The meal in question consisted of a cardboard box in which was stowed a pale and hairy portion of greasy, battery-fed chicken and a number of soggy chips. It was, in short, the sort of mass-produced, Americanized food which tastes at the best of wet blotting-paper and at the worst of very old bicycle tyres: such a dinner as makes me more than ever anxious for the speedy collapse of Civilization As We Know It. Having secured this repellent repast, Simpson paid for it with money from the purse which he always carried about his person and made his way out of the neon-lit splendours of the Delectable Drumstick into the stormy unpleasantness of the street. He was going, as usual, to take the tube to his bed-sitting room in Paddington.

Exactly what followed never became altogether clear. Prosecuting counsel failed to elicit a coherent story from the various witnesses, and the defence was, as usual, only too happy to allow the picture to remain somewhat opaque. As Simpson walked along the broad and fairly well-lit pavement, he passed a large and rather muddy vehicle (it was later shown to be a Volvo estate car with a Hampshire registration) which drew up behind him. A man got out, of no more than Simpson's age but of an entirely different appearance. He was large and burly, a first class Rugby football player, whereas Simpson was on the skinny side and his game, on the rare occasions when he could find a partner, was draughts. The man from the estate car wore a suit made by Huntsman's in Savile Row, a hat from Lock's and made-to-measure shoes from Lobb; Simpson was dressed in a nondescript manner by courtesy of the January sales in the Civil Service Stores. The man from the Volvo was a product of Eton, Sandhurst and the Brigade of Guards; Simpson had acquired his mastery of mathematics at Stanmore Comprehensive and the North London Poly. It would be difficult to think of two more dissimilar young men than Percival Simpson and the Honourable Roderick (known to his many friends as Rory) Canter, younger son of the late Marquess of Freith. And yet they were to be inextricably joined in a famous double act, playing the parts of corpse and defendant in a trial staged before a large public at the Old Bailey.

We can now go conveniently to the evidence of Mr Byron MacDonald, the Jamaican guard of a train which was waiting at the platform of Notting Hill Gate station, bound for Paddington. Mr MacDonald was standing looking out of the open door of his compartment when he saw the fresh-faced Honourable Rory, with his well-cut clothes and general air of a gentleman farmer, come down onto the platform. Mr MacDonald waited for this late passenger to get onto the train, but Rory Canter showed no signs of doing so, and instead moved to a place on the platform where there was a bench set in a kind of small cave of lavatory tiling. He stood in the alcove, as the guard Byron MacDonald shouted, 'Mind the doors please!' and gave the signal for the train to move out of the station.

As the doors shut and the train sighed heavily and lumbered rheumatically forward, Mr MacDonald saw Simpson come onto the platform in his shapeless raincoat, still clutching his plastic dinner-bag, which bore on it the well-known symbol of the Delectable Drumstick. Simpson looked round, and then stepped back towards the alcove where Rory Canter was standing. The last sight that Byron MacDonald saw, as the train carried him off into the darkness of the tunnel, was two apparent strangers struggling together, locked in some inexplicable combat or embrace.

James 'Peanuts' Anderson and Diana 'Smokey' Revere were part of a group of young people who came down to the platform about four minutes later on pleasure bent. They were variously dressed in black leather, safety-pins and a job lot of Iron Crosses and other emblems of the Wehrmacht. Peanuts' cropped hair was of a light green shade and Dianna's was tinted orange. They both wore heavy eye-shadow and, with their companions, were deriving such innocent pleasure as they could from kicking an empty lager can down the stairs and along the platform. From time to time during their progress, they punched or kicked each other in an affectionate manner.

Dianna Smokey Revere remembered seeing the man in the mackintosh move away from the seat on which the man in the trilby hat and the tweed suit was left sitting. At that moment another train came in, the doors opened and the young people kicked their beer can into an empty compartment. They went into the same compartment and milled around at one end, refreshing themselves from other tins of lager which they had brought with them. The girl Smokey remembered seeing Simpson sitting alone at the other end of the carriage, his plastic bag of dinner on the floor between his knees. He was carrying some object, what it was she could not exactly see, but it seemed to her to be about a foot long. She saw him drop it, whatever it was, into the plastic bag, inside which it hit the floor with a metallic clang. Her final view of the platform included the sight of a pale Rory Canter slipping sideways on the seat where he was sitting, so that he hit the lavatory tiles and then slithered to the ground. From the moving train it looked as though he were drunk; and so he seemed not at all out of place on Notting Hill Gate tube station at night.

Smokey, Peanuts and their friends scarcely paid any attention to Simpson when he left the train at Paddington. When he got out of the station, he made a few turnings away from the main thoroughfare into a short cul-de-sac called Alexander Herzen Road. Number 2 was the tall, crumbling, Victorian house which contained his bed-sit. By the stone steps which led up to the front door there was a row of dustbins, round which had gathered the debris left by resentful dustmen who never got a Christmas box. Percival Simpson opened the lid of one of these dustbins and dropped into it his plastic bag of dinner untasted.

When he had done this he seemed somewhat relieved in his mind, and went, as always, up to his room alone.

Although these events might, in the old days, have provided a certain amount of grist to the Rumpole mill, and might have been expected to yield the good things of the earth such as briefs, and money to pay the tax man and my clerk Henry, and the ever-increasing tick at Pommeroy's Wine Bar, and even keep my wife Hilda, known to me in awe as She Who Must Be Obeyed, in Vim for a month or two, they were now as remote from my sphere as the alleged delinquencies of little green men in outer space. At the time when Simpson caught his tube train and left the collapsing Hon. Rory on his bench, I was in a deck chair gently ripening to a roseate hue in the brilliant sunshine of southern Florida, looking out past the golden sand and assorted geriatrics to the Atlantic Ocean. I was in a strange condition which could be described as neither life nor death but something in between; a kind of air-conditioned purgatory. Not to put too fine a point on it, I had retired and gone to live in America.

The summons to this lotus-eating existence had come from my son, Nick, always the brains of the family, who had crowned his academic career by becoming Head of the Department of Social Studies in the University of Miami. He had also acquired a sizeable house with a swimming bath in the garden, a place which his wife Erica mysteriously referred to as the 'back yard'. When I add that Erica was expecting the Rumpole grandchild, and that Nick was constantly arguing that the time had come for me to hang up my old wig, give up the unequal struggle against the forces of law and order and join him and his wife in a sun-blessed haven far from the piercing draughts of our old mansion flat in Gloucester Road, and the cold winds and brutal proceedings of the Uxbridge Magistrates Court, you will understand why my wife Hilda was naturally and persistently in favour of this scheme. However, she would never have persuaded me if it hadn't been for the powerful argument advanced by his Honour Judge Roger Bullingham.

I lost ten cases in a row before Judge Bullingham. Bullingham, or the mad Bull, was, some years ago, elevated from his relative obscurity in the London Sessions to perform in the more popular arena of the Central Criminal Court. Far from maturing into any sort of civilization, the Bull relapsed into a deeper barbarity in his new post. He growled savagely at witnesses, he shouted and reduced young male barristers to stammering jellies and made lady barristers weep (Miss Trant, the Portia of our Chambers, once fled in tears from Bullingham's Court, saying that the cause of justice there would be advanced if they brought back trial by ordeal). He smiled with crawling sycophancy at juries, commiserated with them on the length of defence cross-examinations and told them the Test Match score, hoping to woo them to a conviction. During defence speeches he slept ostentatiously, or explored his ear with his little finger, or industriously picked his nose. When welfare officers suggested probation, he trumpeted with contempt; when police officers gave their evidence of improbable verbal admissions, he passed it on to the jury with the solemnity of Moses relaying the Tablets of the Law. His sentences were invariably greeted with outbursts of hysterical weeping by women in the public gallery.

I have always said that if you could choose your judge you could win most cases, and to avoid this undesirable result the authorities award judges to cases by some mysterious system of chance. The night before a case your clerk tells you which judge you have drawn in the lottery, and when I got his Honour Judge Bullingham for the tenth time I felt like some Monte Carlo gambler who, against all the odds, faces a record run on the black, leading to bankruptcy and a pistol shot on the terrace. All the same, my client was a Post Office worker of hitherto unblemished reputation, his wife was suffering from a long illness and the amount he was alleged to have fiddled was no more than two hundred pounds. The Bull, however, was at his worst. He fawned on the jury, constantly interrupted my cross-examination and forced me to make my final speech on Friday afternoon, so that the jury would have forgotten it by Monday morning when he made the ferocious prosecution plea which he called his summing-up. The jury obediently convicted, and my back and head were aching as I heaved myself to my hind legs in a vain attempt to appeal to the Bull's better nature in the matter of sentence. Eventually I subsided with the familiar Bull phrases ringing in my ears: 'Very serious crime ... Gross breach of trust by a public servant ... It is quite inappropriate for counsel to ask for leniency in this class of case ... Post Office frauds are going to be stamped out as far as this Court is concerned ... The least sentence I can pass is one of four years' imprisonment ...'

My client's daughter sobbed in the public gallery as he was led down to the cells. 'And the least sentence I can pass on you, Bull,' I said, only just under my breath, 'is banishment for life. Avaunt and quit my sight. Let the earth hide thee. Thy bones are marrowless, thy blood is cold. Thou hast no speculation in those eyes that thou dost glare with!' and a good deal more to the like effect. It was clear, of course, that the only way I could really banish Judge Bullingham from my life was to hang up my wig and leave the Old Bailey for ever. So we accepted Nick's invitation and moved to southern Florida.

On our shopping days, after a somewhat insubstantial and teeth-freezing lunch of a mountainous salad (jumbo prawns, inflatable tomatoes, Icelandic lettuce – the stuff to avoid is 'Thousand Island Dressing': so many islands, you might have thought, are hardly needed to provide a mixture of salad cream and tomato ketchup), Hilda and I would take chairs on the beach and go through the back numbers of *The Times* that my old friend George Frobisher posted to us from time to time. Around us 'Senior Citizens', old men wearing long shorts, peaked cotton caps and eye shields, antique ladies whose shrunken arms and necks were loaded with jewellery, sat blinking in the sun or queued for the three dollar blood pressure service which was available to warn of a sudden heart attack as the Dow Jones average plummeted, or the microchip in charge of our destinies mischievously ordered up a nuclear war.

'That *is* nice,' said She Who Must Be Obeyed, clucking approvingly at her copy of *The Times*. 'Queen's Birthday Honours go to Mrs Whitehouse and Margaret Thatcher's milkman.'

There are moments when I scarcely regret my exile from England, and this was one of them. But then I began to read the account of an unsolved London crime: ' "Notting Hill Gate

Mystery. The Honourable Rory Canter, younger brother of Lord Freith and wealthy Hampshire landowner, stabbed in underground station." My God. It *is* a mystery. What's an Honourable doing down the tube, like a common barrister?'

The smile put on it by the elevation of the Prime Minister's milkman faded from Hilda's face.

'I wish you'd stop worrying about that sort of thing, Rumpole, now I've persuaded you to retire.'

'You didn't persuade me to retire. His Honour Judge Bullingham persuaded me to retire. Anyway, I was losing my touch. I couldn't've shovelled more customers into Wandsworth if I'd joined the Old Bill.' I tried to forget Bullingham by reading the account of a more or less decent crime. ' "Mr Canter had abandoned his Volvo estate car and gone down the underground." The Honourable gentleman must have been a tube-spotter.'

'I think Nick and I rescued you from murders just in time, Rumpole. You were looking distinctly seedy.'

'Not half as seedy as my clients. I'd leave the Temple every night, like Napoleon making a quick retreat from Moscow, abandoning the dead and dying to their fate ...'

'You should be grateful to Nick. Thanks to him we shall have Christmas in this wonderful climate.'

I looked up at the relentlessly blue sky for signs of rain. 'Excellent climate, I'm sure,' I told Hilda, 'if you happen to be an orange.'

'And Nick's inviting his university friends over for a barbecue tonight. Poolside,' Hilda reminded me. It was true that my son had acquired a strange habit of cooking meals on a sort of camp-fire beside the swimming bath. 'The Professor of Law's coming. You'll have someone to talk to.'

'What can I say? I'm not a lawyer ... any more.' I looked back, a little puzzled, at the *Times* account of the Notting Hill Gate murder. 'Now why should a man abandon his Volvo estate car and dive down the tube ...? Oh well ... Never mind! It can't possibly be my business any more. Rumpole's occupation's gone.'

'What did you say, Rumpole?'

'Nothing, Hilda. Nothing at all.' I closed my eyes and tried to rewrite *Othello*.

'Farewell the Ancient Court,
Farewell the wiggéd troup and the old Judge,
That made oppression virtue. Oh farewell,
Pride, pomp and circumstance of glorious London Sessions . . .'

By this time I felt further pangs of nostalgia, even at the mention of that desolate courthouse down past the Elephant and Castle. So I tried to remember the things I missed least about my life in the law: such as Bullingham passing sentence and Chambers meetings, presided over by my learned ex-Head of Chambers, Guthrie Featherstone, Q.C., M.P.

Chapter Two

At about the time that I was reading the prodigiously delayed account of the Notting Hill Underground Murder Mystery, the evening peace of the Temple was shattered by the roar of a powerful motor-bicycle and a figure, hugely helmeted and dressed from neck to ankle in black leather, astride an over-powered Japanese Honda, came thundering in through the Embankment gates, waved a gauntleted greeting at the startled porter on duty and did a racing turn into Kings Bench Walk, narrowly missing a collision with the hearse-like vintage Daim-ler of a Lord of Appeal in Ordinary. The Dirt Track Rider screamed to a halt, dismounted and unfastened a black briefcase from his pillion. He then proceeded on foot towards Equity Court, where my old Chambers is situated.

Entering Number Two, the Speedway King passed the door on which the list of familiar names was painted. Guthrie Featherstone, Q.C., M.P., led all the rest, beating by a short head the name Horace Rumpole, which had been crossed out in biro, the Temple sign-painter having never got around to paint-ing it out and moving the other names, Thomas Cartwright (Uncle Tom), Judge George Frobisher, Claude Erskine-Brown, Phillida Trant (who has now, in the make-believe world of married life, adopted the pseudonym of Mrs Erskine-Brown), Clement Hoskins, Flavius Quint, etc., etc. The motor-bicyclist, who had now removed the huge plastic balloon from his head and emerged as a reasonably good-looking young man of thirty with a tumbling lock of black hair, thick eyebrows and the ex-pression of one who constantly believes that he is about to be insulted and doesn't intend to stand for it, glanced at the list of names, as he had done on many occasions, appeared to notice a glaring omission and continued on into the clerk's room, looking more resentful than ever.

As it was six thirty my ex-clerk Henry, whom I can remember as a barely literate office boy, was just leaving to take our typist Dianne for their customary Cinzano Bianco in Pommeroy's, where they lit each other's cigarettes, occasionally held hands when they thought no one was looking, and tried to delay, for as long as possible, the inevitable journey home to their respective spouses. Henry is now touching forty, his hair no longer covers his ears, his trousers are less flared and his suits more conservative: he is beginning to look like a man with the sort of income a young barrister might aspire to only after years of practice. He watched without expression as the biker undid a multitude of zips, shed his skin of leather and emerged, like a somewhat formal snake, in a grey suit.

'Mind if I hang my gear on your door, Henry? Being a squatter gives you no damn place to put anything.'

He looked at my ex-clerk as if expecting some reactionary opposition to his plan, which he would be able to denounce on a point of democratic principle. He seemed almost disappointed when Henry's only reply was, 'That's quite all right, Mr Cracknell. The Chambers meeting's being going on about ten minutes.'

The man addressed as Cracknell raised his eyes to the ceiling above which, in Featherstone's room, the established members of Chambers were discussing matters of great importance, particularly to him.

'This Chambers meeting is the first we have held in the absence of a once familiar figure . . .'

Guthrie Featherstone was in the chair, behaving with his customary mixture of self-assurance and nervousness, as if constantly aware that things might all get terribly out of hand (I owe my knowledge of this meeting to Miss Phillida Trant, the Portia of our Chambers, who described it all to me much, much later).

'Rumpole!' It was my old friend George Frobisher, now a Circuit (or as I prefer to call it, Circus) Judge who guessed that Featherstone, in his somewhat elliptical way, was referring to the Old Bailey Hack, now put out to grass in a distant land.

'I understand a card has been dispatched to carry our joint

greetings to Horace Rumpole in his well-deserved retirement,' Featherstone told them and smiled. 'No doubt the cost has been deducted from Chambers' expenses.'

'We thought we'd never get rid of Rumpole. We kept giving him farewell dinners,' Uncle Tom grumbled. No doubt he remembered the clock they all gave me once in the hope of putting me out to grass, a suggestion which, on that occasion, I made bold to resist. Then up spoke a diminutive, grey-haired Welshman with an insinuating voice and the look of a man who could apply a good deal of low cunning to running-down cases. He was a practitioner on the Welsh Circuit named Owen Glendour-Owen and a recent addition to Chambers.

'The man's lucky to have a son doing well at a foreign university, from what I can gather. Very comfortable billet he must have there now.'

'All the same, Chambers doesn't seem Chambers without Rumpole.' My old friend George Frobisher put in a word for me.

'Exactly! We seem to have got rid of the stink of cheap, small cigars in the passages.' Claude Erskine-Brown, never one of the Rumpole fan club, had no regrets.

'There do seem to be rather fewer villains loitering about Chambers,' George admitted.

And Uncle Tom, our oldest, and absolutely briefless member of Chambers (he comes in every day to read the law reports, do the *Times* crossword and get away from the unmarried sister who polishes violently round him if he stays at home) came out with one of his interminable reminiscences. 'I seem to recall,' he said, 'that one of Rumpole's clients took up the waiting-room carpet before a conference. And removed it in a hold-all!'

Featherstone smiled round at the conspirators, who seemed to be agreeing that they were better off without Rumpole. 'And I don't have the embarrassment of judges raising the question of Rumpole's hat – as a disgrace to the legal profession! However, I digress.' He got down to business. 'Rumpole's final retirement, much delayed as Uncle Tom reminds us ...'

He kept making his positively last appearance,' Uncle Tom suggested, quite unnecessarily, 'like a bloody opera singer!'

'Rumpole's final departure' – Featherstone was now in full flood – 'has left a considerable gap in our ranks. In fact you may say that the loss of one Rumpole has made room for at least two other members of the Bar. We have been fortunate indeed that Owen Glendour-Owen has joined us from Cardiff, with his useful connection with car insurance.'

The addition of this cunning Celt, which might have been greeted with cries of despair in happier days, now seemed an occasion of deep satisfaction to my treacherous ex-colleagues. There were murmurs of approval, cries of 'Welcome, Owen' and 'Hear, hear!', at which the tiny Welshman twinkled complacently and told them proudly, 'They call me "Knock-for-Knock" Owen in the valleys.'

Featherstone called the meeting to order. 'I thought I'd take this opportunity,' he said, 'to raise the question of the other candidate who might share Rumpole's old room with you, Glendour-Owen. As you all know, young Cracknell has been with us during the past year as a squatter ...'

Here, perhaps, I should explain a legal term. The average young man, hopeful of pursuing a brilliant career at the Bar, may think that he is brought to the 'Off' simply by passing his exams, eating his dinners, getting 'called' by his Inn and doing his six months' pupillage in the Chambers of some established practitioner. If he thinks this, he's in for an unpleasant surprise. Once his pupillage is over, he may well be flung out of the Chambers and left with nowhere to park his backside or put his briefs on the mantelpiece. He is without a clerk to send him rushing out for ten quid to Uxbridge Magistrates Court, and he hasn't even the corner of a room to hold a decent conference. In short, our young hopeful cannot start to practise until he finds some set of Chambers to take him in. Accordingly he clings on to his place of pupillage with the tenacity of a drowning man clutching an overcrowded raft: although he knows he is unwanted, and there is probably not enough ship's biscuits and water to go round, he prefers to hang on rather than brave the dark and hostile waters around him. An ex-pupil in this position is called a 'squatter'; he turns up at Chambers every day like a perpetual rebuke, does his work in some inconvenient corner and will continue to squat on until he's either pushed off to sink or swim somewhere else in the Temple, or accepted (as he devoutly hopes) as a permanent tenant with a right to sit at a desk, be clerked by Henry, typed for by Dianne and raise his voice at Chambers meetings. And since my retirement there had arrived to squat at Number Two Equity Court none other than the Dirt Track Rider himself, young Kenneth Cracknell.

'Cracknell? Is that the fellow that looks as though he's dropped in from Mars?' George sounded disapproving.

'I saw him in the clerk's room the other day. I thought he'd come to deliver a telegram.' Erskine-Brown was scarcely more enthusiastic.

'Oh, I know you're all against Ken.' Phillida Trant looked round at the male members of Chambers in a defensive fashion.

'Ken?' George wondered. 'Is Ken the person from outer space?'

'Cracknell gets a fair amount of work. He's about to do a long fraud with Phillida Trant, and a dirty books case in the north.' Glendour-Owen seemed to have a more intimate acquaintance with the squatter, whom he seemed to see as a potential money-spinner.

'Do we really *want* dirty books in Chambers?' Erskine-Brown sounded unimpressed.

'Probably a good deal more amusing than the Law Reports.' Uncle Tom put the other side of the argument.

Featherstone smiled round at them all; but he smiled most at the lady I shall always remember as Miss Phillida Trant. He thought she was looking particularly beautiful, flushed with opposition to the oppressive anti-Cracknell faction which included her husband. Featherstone had never been entirely able to understand why the proudly beautiful Miss Trant, whose appearance in wig and gown, stiff collar, white bands and horn-rimmed specs was one, to his mind, of flagrant sexuality, had been snatched off and put in pod by Claude Erskine-Brown who, by any sensible board of selectors, would undoubtedly be chosen to bore for England. Featherstone, in spite of his appearance of respectability and his longing for the High Court Bench, was frequently troubled by pangs of ill-directed love, of the sort that had brought him so near to disaster in the case of Angela, our temporary Trotskyite typist.* As he saw Miss Trant

* See 'Rumpole and the Case of Identity' in *The Trials of Rumpole*, Penguin Books, 1979.

glaring with hostility at her husband, Featherstone felt the stimulating tremor of a marriage breaking up and resolved to lose no opportunity in inviting Miss Trant to lunch. He also decided to throw his weight on her side in the Cracknell controversy.

'Interesting fellow, Cracknell,' Featherstone said. 'He tells me that he intends to do cases connected with civil rights.'

'Exactly!' Erskine-Brown sounded as though his worst fears were confirmed. Miss Trant looked at her husband with a hostility that made Featherstone's heart flutter.

'Well, what's wrong with civil rights? Better than civil wrong, wouldn't you say so? Of course, Ken's a radical lawyer. I know that's the sort you don't want to have the key of the lavatory ... like women and blacks!' She started her usual oration, and her husband looked at her, puzzled.

'Philly, what on earth's come over you?'

'Blacks! That reminds me ...' Uncle Tom had somewhat lost the thread of the argument. 'They nearly wished a Parsee on us once. I voted for you, old fellow.' He slapped a surprised Glendour-Owen on the shoulder. 'Even though you're Welsh.'*

'Well, I'm not sure Cracknell sounds in the least bit desirable.' Erskine-Brown looked at his wife. 'From what you tell me, Philly, he lives in a commune.'

'I told you, Claude, that he lives in a community. Near King's Cross.' His wife corrected him and went on, flushed with sincerity, 'I've seen Ken once or twice in action. Down at Bow Street. Believe it or not, he's a very attractive advocate.'

At which point the door opened and the squatter entered. The others looked somewhat startled, as if they'd been caught out in some discreditable conspiracy. Miss Phillida Trant was the first to greet him, using that shortened version of his Christian name which he insisted on to show that he was of radical views, a man of the people, totally without pretensions, and not a pompous barrister like the rest of us.

'Oh, hello, Ken,' said Miss Trant, almost shyly.

'Well, hullo.' Young Cracknell looked round the room, unsmiling. 'Aren't squatters invited?'

'Of course.' Featherstone was almost too effusive. 'And you

* See 'Rumpole and the Fascist Beast' in the same volume.

won't be a squatter forever. We're considering the position of accommodation in Chambers, now that Rumpole's left.'

'Rumpole?' Ken Cracknell seemed genuinely puzzled. 'Everyone's always talking about Rumpole. I've never met the man.'

Chapter Three

'It's a sunshine day.'

'Well, as a matter of fact, it always is.'

I was standing on the 'sidewalk' of a busy shopping street in Miami; around me the population were busily Dunkin' Doughnuts or chewing Happy Brunchburgers, or pushing overburdened trolleys filled with convenience foods, or merely standing on the street corners of Dade City (it's a little-known fact that the late Colonel Dade was actually defeated by the Red Indians) hoping, in an unconvinced sort of way, for Good Times Just Around The Corner. I had bought a new box of small cigars, Hilda was waiting for me in a battered yellow taxi, and I was confronted with an unusual sight in that bustling city, where the young people looked as if they'd just swum in from Cuba and the old people looked anxiously embalmed, of a young man wearing a quiet tie, a clean white shirt, well-ironed jeans and industriously polished shoes. His hair was short, clean and neatly parted. He was proffering to me, held between finger and thumb, a large yellow flower, which looked, considering the surrounding petrol fumes and the humidity, surprisingly perky.

'A sunshine day for you and me, friend and brother,' the young man repeated. 'Praise to the Eternal Sun!'

I had been thinking for weeks of the soft rain falling round the Temple tube station, but I didn't want to argue. As politeness seemed to demand it, I took his chrysanth. In a tone of voice which sounded quite practical he announced that he had something more to offer.

'Want to take a hand-out?' he said. He had a bunch of pamphlets, in favour of what? Strip shows, life insurance, cut-price burial or the protection of whales?

'Are you selling something?' I asked him.

'Sunlight!' The young man was smiling at me. I thought he

might be a salesman for picture windows or patio doors. Whatever sort of sunlight he was dealing in, I imagined it came at a fair old price.

I opened the taxi door and was about to get in beside Hilda when he said, 'Meet and talk?'

'What?'

'We shall meet and talk, friend and brother. As sure as the seeds grow in the sunlight. We shall meet and talk ...'

'Sorry. Got to get back home now. My son Nick's giving a party. Poolside.'

I shut the taxi door then, but I still saw his pleasant face, framed in the open window. He raised his hand in a sort of cheerful salute and said, 'Sunlight to Children of Sun! Blood to Children of Dark!'

As the taxi moved away I returned the friendliest greeting I could think of. 'And a very Happy Christmas to you too.'

'Rumpole,' said She Who Must Be Obeyed. 'You're holding a flower.'

'Well, so I am.'

'He seemed a very nice young man,' Hilda said. 'He looked so very different from most young people nowadays.'

She was smiling, so I gave her the flower. She sniffed it enthusiastically and then put it on the seat beside her, where it wilted in the long traffic jam going out of the city.

' "Meet and talk." A total stranger came up to me in the city, gave me a chrysanth and said, "Meet and talk." '

'It may seem just crazy to you, Dad,' my daughter-in-law said, giving me that sweet smile of toleration for the Senior Citizen which I find particularly irritating, 'but people around here just like to rap on ... about life, and God and such like.' Erica was wrapped in some sort of ethnic, handwoven garment which did little to conceal the fact that she was expecting the first Rumpole ever to become a citizen of the United States. 'Maybe now you've given up the rat race you'll learn to rap with strangers, Dad.'

It grated a little, I must confess, to hear all the real world I once inhabited, the cloud-capped Assize Courts, the golden pinnacles of the Old Bailey itself, the Lords of Appeal and the

Great Villains, the Circus Judges and the Timson family (notorious crooks of South London), my notable trials including the Penge Bungalow Murders and the Great Grimsby Fish Fraud, all referred to as the rat race. I looked at Nick, my son, who had the brazier going on which he proposed to cook large steaks, which would be served with salad and glasses of Californian wine (not really *much* worse than Pommeroy's plonk) when the guests arrived. I remembered that the last time I had seen him cook out of doors was when he was about eight and we boiled shrimps over a camp-fire on the beach at Lowestoft. And then the chime of bells sounded at Nick's front door and he went in through the house to receive his visitors.

'I guess you'll be able to make your own space now you're retired, Dad.' Erica was often difficult to follow. 'You'll really be able to find yourself.'

'I don't know about that,' I said when I'd thought the matter over. 'I might not like myself after I'd found me.'

At which point Nick came back to the camp-fire with the guests for the evening: Professor Nathan Blowfield, Head of the Legal Faculty (a small, round man in a tartan jacket whose health was in constant danger owing to his indulgence in the habit of jogging), and his wife Betsy Blowfield, both of whom I knew already; and a couple who were strangers to me, a very pretty and smiling black girl in a white silk shirt, clean dungarees and gold glasses, and her attendant male, a supervisor from the English Department. Their names were announced as Paul Gilpin and Tiffany Jones.

'Any time you want to come up to the campus, Mr Rumpole,' Professor Blowfield smiled invitingly, 'I'm sure my students would be honoured to meet a trial lawyer from England.'

'Am I a trial lawyer?' I asked him. 'I used to think I'd passed the test.'

'Tell me,' young Paul Gilpin looked at me with amusement, 'do you guys still wear the rug ...?' He patted the top of his head. 'What do you call it, the peruke? In your courtrooms ...'

'I have hung up my old wig.' I downed a sizeable gulp of the Californian claret-style. 'Rumpole's occupation's gone. But yes. I wore my crown of itchy horsehair for almost half a century.'

'And I'm sure you looked real nice in it.' Tiffany Jones was smiling at me; she seemed a pleasant girl whose serious spectacles and matter-of-fact American voice belied her exotic, African appearance. 'You must have looked like George Washington or something.'

'If that was the old darling who never told a lie,' I had to admit, 'well really, not much.'

'Nick tells us you're retired now,' Paul Gilpin said.

'Yes. I dropped out. I bought this sunshine shirt.' I had, in fact, invested in a Miami shirting which was about as discreet as the eruption of Vesuvius. 'And Hilda and I spend our days bumming round the beach.'

'You've found time to breathe a little?' Paul Gilpin asked me in a meaningful sort of way.

'I used to breathe down the Old Bailey,' I told him, 'strange as it may seem.'

'I guess Paul only meant that you'd found peace of mind, since your retirement.' The others had wandered away in search of food and drink and I was left with Tiffany Jones, whose gentle voice made me feel that I had been unnecessarily rude to the well-meaning Paul.

'I'm not sure peace of mind interests me exactly. You see,' I did my best to explain, 'after a life of crime, I suppose I'm finding it difficult to go straight.' Again she made me feel I was talking too much about myself, and even wallowing in *nostalgie de l'*Old Bailey. She seemed a particularly nice girl, and I wanted to find out more about her. 'What department are you in up at the University, Miss ... Jones?'

'Oh please, "Tiffany".' She put a long-fingered brown hand on my arm as she spoke, and I avoided looking for any reaction from She Who Must Be Obeyed. 'I'm in social economics and statistics.' It had to be admitted that the confession was not romantic, although the manner in which she made it was. 'I've always had a head for figures. Since I was a kid, I guess. I cover the economic statistics for Nick's Department of Sociology.'

'How many one-parent families in inner-city areas take to pinching milk bottles.' I knew what she meant: I once had a twelve-year-old delinquent for a client who told me his trouble was he couldn't 'relate to his mother in a one-to-one supportive relationship'.

27

'That kind of thing.' Tiffany grinned. 'I like the statistics ... but the rest of it's a lot of crap, isn't it? I mean, wherever you come from, you can always choose between God and the Devil.' Although she was still looking happy and radiant, her words had a sudden, almost chilling seriousness.

'Can we choose?' I asked her. 'Fate dealt me an old devil called Judge Bullingham for ten cases running.'

'No matter what luck you have, there's always a choice between light and darkness. The choice is yours, as sure as the seed grows in the sunshine.'

I frowned, trying to remember. Her words troubled me, like an unfamiliar quotation; but when she spoke again, of course, I got the source immediately.

'We must meet and talk on this subject, friend and brother,' Tiffany Jones said. 'You and I must meet and talk.'

'Did you hear that, Rumpole?' Hilda interrupted from the middle distance. I looked down and noticed, with mingled regret and relief, that Tiffany's hand had left my arm. 'Erica says it's wonderful to feel that we don't have to rush off back to England. Haven't you got anything to say to that?'

'Have you got anything to say, why sentence of death should not be passed upon you?' Her words had put me in mind of an old legal anecdote, and as Professor Blowfield was then re-filling my glass with Château Vieux Frontier, or whatever strange name it went by, I decided to give him the benefit of it. 'I'll tell you a bit of law, Professor. A bit of legal history ...'

'I sure wish my students could hear it, Mr Rumpole.'

'He was a devil!' I told them. 'The old Lord Chief Justice! When I was first at the Bar. An enormously unlovable character. Used to order muffins for tea at his Club after passing death sentences. Anyway, this old Lord Chief was about to pass sentence in his usual manner ...'

'I'm going to get your husband to give a seminar to the Law Faculty,' I heard Professor Blowfield tell Hilda with some pride, to which she answered shortly, 'That's very thoughtful of you, Professor Blowfield. But I do want Rumpole to rest.'

Undeterred I battled on with the anecdote. 'And the clerk of the Court intoned, "Have you anything to say why sentence of death should not be passed upon you?" "Bugger all, my

Lord," the murderer muttered. Whereupon the old Lord Chief turned to this murderer's counsel, a nervous sort of individual called Bleaks. "Did your client say something, Mr Bleaks?" "Bugger all, my Lord", Bleaks stammered. "That's distinctly odd," grunted the old Lord Chief. "I could've sworn I heard him *say* something." '

I can't say the Rumpole comic turn brought a standing ovation. I laughed, as I have for years at that particular story, and I was flattered to find that Tiffany laughed with me. Nick made an effort and smiled; Hilda also made an effort and didn't. Paul Gilpin, the Blowfields and Erica all looked seriously puzzled.

'Poor old Nick,' I said, feeling sorry for my son. 'He was brought up on that story. That story was "Goldilocks and the Three Bears" to my son Nicholas.'

Professor Blowfield cleared his throat. He had, it seemed, decided to open the seminar. 'Mr Rumpole, in your experience, what was the most important case in Britain during your long career?'

That was an easy one, and I had no doubt at all as to the answer. 'The most important case was undoubtedly the Penge Bungalow Murders.'

'The Penge Bungalow? What did that decide exactly?' The Professor tried in vain to recall his legal textbooks.

'It decided,' I told him, 'that I was able to win a murder, alone and without a leader. It was the start – of the Rumpole career.'

'Did it turn on a nice point of law?' the Professor asked eagerly.

'Law?' I had to disillusion him. 'There was no law about it. It turned on a nice point of blood.'

Chapter Four

Blood, of course, was to prove the undoing of Percival Simpson; blood and the fact that he possessed an extremely observant landlady who had never liked him and had always found his natural shyness and reserve deeply suspicious. As I was giving Professor Blowfield a Golden Oldie from my collection of legal anecdotes, Simpson was coming down the stairs of his lodgings in Alexander Herzen Road with his mackintosh over his arm to meet the inquisitive landlady hoovering in the hall.

'Just slipping out to the cleaners, Mrs O'Dwyer.' Simpson said it in a half-hearted attempt at friendliness, but the unsolicited information immediately attracted her attention to the mackintosh over his arm, and to what seemed to her to be, although faintly, a pinkish stain only half hidden by a fold in the cloth. So, as soon as her lodger was safely out of the house, Mrs O'Dwyer abandoned her Hoover and went up to his room for a good look round. She saw what she had often seen, and disapproved of, on previous visits when she did her minimal cleaning. On Simpson's dressing-table was a crude and amateurish watercolour, cheaply framed, of a naked couple, hands stretched upwards towards a flaming yellow sun in a deep-blue sky. Beside it was, also framed, the coloured portrait photograph of a cleric with crinkly white hair, kindly eyes beaming behind rimless glasses and a deep and healthy suntan. In front of the photograph stood, in a votive position, a half-burned candle in a china holder; beside it lay an ornately handled and curved Moroccan dagger in a bronze sheath, and, carefully folded and kept in place by the handle of the dagger, was a square of white paper through which some scrawled, red lettering was just visible.

Mrs O'Dwyer looked at this collection, the only pool of colour in the drab room, and saw nothing that she had not seen before. She looked at the narrow divan-bed with its porridge-coloured hessian bedspread, and the shelf over it on which were lodged a Bible and several volumes on revenue law, together with a tattered copy of *The House at Pooh Corner*, a relic of Simpson's childhood. Then she opened the wardrobe. There were very few clothes hanging in it: an old jacket, a suit for very best, a few shirts and underclothes; but Mrs O'Dwyer looked down at a pile of dirty washing at the bottom of the cupboard. She picked up a shirt and looked at the cuff, and there she found, to her considerable excitement and enormous satisfaction, a stain that was a deeper pink, in which the attempt at washing had been less successful than the mark on the mackintosh that her secretive lodger had been taking to the cleaners. She went straight down to the hall and lifted the telephone.

The wail of police sirens is not an unknown noise around Alexander Herzen Road near Paddington. The neighbours paid only casual attention to the posse of uniformed officers and to the police dogs nosing round the area's steps. No one saw the treasure that dogs and men recovered from one of the dustbins: a plastic bag from the Delectable Drumstick inside which, beside a box of mouldering chicken, lay an army sheath knife, found, on forensic examination, to be liberally stained with blood of the same group as that which once flowed in the veins of the Honourable Rory Canter. When he returned to the house and found police officers waiting for him, Percival Simpson smiled a little wearily, but did not seem at all surprised.

The officers in charge of the Notting Hill Gate Underground Murder were led by Detective Inspector Wargrave, a friendly and comfortable-looking copper who sang bass-baritone in the Gilbert and Sullivan put on by his local operatic society and always cast himself as the Dutch uncle in interviews. Young Detective Constable Jarwood, on the other hand, was pale, sharp-featured and unsmiling, and conducted interviews as if the responsibility of fighting crime rested on him alone.

'Want a cup of tea, lad, do you?' D.I. Wargrave started the interrogation of Simpson with the soft approach.

'I know,' the arrested man looked at the D.I. as though he hadn't heard, 'I have sinned.'

'You're telling us you're guilty, then?' D.C. Jarwood sounded almost disappointed as he made a note; like an eager huntsman who sees the fox come trotting up to the meet and lie down. Simpson seemed to have fallen into a sort of reverie from which the D.I. sought to awaken him.

'How long have you known him, Percy?'

'How long have you known the Honourable Rory Canter?' Jarwood repeated the question, more insistently. 'The one you cut.'

Simpson shook his head and said, quite gently, 'I didn't know him.'

'Don't lie to us, Simpson,' the Detective Constable came in dead on cue.

'It's true. I'd never seen him before.' Simpson sounded as if he didn't really care whether they believed him or not. 'Of course, I knew he'd come ... sometime.'

'So you went after him?' Jarwood asked.

'No!' Simpson said it quite positively; but then he sighed and added, 'What's the use? They'll never let me escape now. Never!'

At which point the Detective Inspector took a plastic envelope from a file and carefully withdrew from it the folded sheet of paper he had found on Simpson's dressing-table, on which a curious message had been printed in blotchy and uneven capitals.

'This in your handwriting, Percy?' Simpson nodded his head, making no attempt to deny it.

'Strange sort of letter, isn't it?' Jarvis suggested.

'Perhaps. To you.' Simpson's interest in the proceedings seemed hard to retain.

'It's written in blood, isn't it, Percy?' Wargrave said it as though he were inviting Simpson to another cup of tea. 'We had the forensic on it, you see. You wrote this in the blood of the gentleman you knifed.'

At which Simpson looked up at him surprised, and for the first time since the interview began he seemed to be genuinely afraid. 'No! Not his blood. Unless ...' He looked at the sheet of paper almost in awe. 'Something miraculous!'

'You're lying to us again, Percy. That's no use to you, you

know.' Jarwood's reaction was predictable, but Simpson looked at him without dissent.

'Of course,' he nodded. 'Nothing's any use. They've got the power! I can't fight it.'

'It's just no good. He can't fight it. He tells the police he's guilty. The bloody knife's in the dustbin. He's identified by at least three witnesses at the tube station and he writes some spooky letter in his victim's blood. The case is as dead as mutton.'

'Just the sort of case Rumpole would have enjoyed.'

In due course Percival Simpson had made his first appearance in the Magistrates Court; it was a short and silent appearance as far as he was concerned and he seemed to show little interest in the proceedings. He was, as was inevitable on a murder charge, granted legal aid and his case was passed to an eager young solicitor, Labour councillor and leading light of the local Law Centre called Michael, or Mike, Mowbray. Mike knew Ken Cracknell (they had been fellow students at the London School of Economics) and, as anxious to advance his friend's career as his own, he gave the brief in this desirable murder (the sort of case for which in my early years at the Bar I would have been tempted to go out and do the deed myself) to the ex-squatter, Dirt Track Rider, now tenant of my old room, K. Cracknell, Esq. Cracknell, although naturally excited as he undid the pink tape which bound the important brief, became increasingly depressed as he calculated the odds stacked against the defence. So he was now sitting in Rex's Café, opposite the Old Bailey, eating some of the superb scrambled eggs that they serve there from dawn on, telling his troubles to the Portia of our Chambers, Mrs Phillida Erskine-Brown (née Trant).

As for Miss Trant, she had taken to setting out from home early, leaving the feeding of the Erskine-Brown infant in the hands of her husband and a large and unsmiling au pair from Iceland who would, as Miss Trant feared, give notice if she gave her the opportunity of the briefest conversation. 'Got to read a brief for 10.30,' Miss Trant would call over her shoulder as she fled the domestic scene. 'I'll grab a cup of coffee at Rex's.'

And off she would go, leaving the child, her husband Claude and Miss Reykjavik to form a gloomy and abandoned alliance. It may also be said that her step lightened as she put an increasing distance between herself and family life in South Kensington, not only because she loved her work, which she did, but because she had grown agreeably used to breakfast with Ken Cracknell, who looked this morning, with his dark hair and smouldering eyes, like a young Heathcliff of the legal aid system.

'Just my luck!' Cracknell continued to complain. 'I thought I'd do my first murder on my own and score a triumphant victory. Now ... no way! I'll be a triumphant loser.'

'That letter ... !' Miss Trant had eagerly and helpfully read her friend Ken Cracknell's brief and had seen the photostat of the strange missive that Percy Simpson appeared to have written in his victim's blood.

'The jury's going to love that!' Cracknell filled his mouth with scrambled egg on a slice and chewed bitterly. 'He doesn't only knife a member of the aristocracy, he uses him as an inkwell to write his correspondence.' Ken looked, if possible, more savagely depressed. 'It's a case that's going to do my career at the Bar no sort of good at all.'

Miss Trant looked at him, smiled and put a hand on his arm. 'I must say, Ken,' she said, 'you're frightfully ambitious. For a radical lawyer.'

'Even radical lawyers are meant to win their cases.' He looked at her, pleased with her obvious concern. 'Why don't we have a hamburger tonight and talk about it. I could show you the commune.'

'I can't, Ken, honestly.' Miss Trant sounded genuinely disappointed. 'My husband'll have dinner all ready. He's started to cook French traditional from the *Observer* colour supplement.'

'Ring him and say you've been kept late in Chambers. A late con.'

'No, I can't. Another time.' She squeezed his arm and let it go, so she could deal better with her marmalade and double toast.

'Another time. You promise?' Ken Cracknell smiled, the effect of which upon Miss Trant was powerful.

'All right. I promise,' she said. She lit a thoughtful, low tar, filter-tipped and quite tasteless cigarette, and added thoughtfully, 'Ken. About that defence of yours ... There *is* someone who really knows about blood stains.'

'You mean Professor Andrew Ackerman?' Cracknell mentioned the Prince of the Morgues, the best forensic science witness in the business. 'He's giving evidence for the prosecution.'

'No.' And Miss Trant breathed out smoke through elegantly flaring nostrils. 'But someone as good as Ackerman. I could write to him, if you like.'

Chapter Five

'Dear Rumpole. It seems ages since you left us and of course we all miss you.' My correspondent, as an advocate, was more ready to say what she thought the tribunal might like to hear than to stick to the strict truth; but let that pass. 'We have got a new fellow in Chambers though, a rather super bloke called Ken Cracknell (he's always called Ken, which shows that there's simply no side or snobbery about him). He always defends, or appears for, tenants, or Indian teachers in front of the Race Relations Boards, and all that sort of thing. In fact, Ken's a real radical lawyer, just like you used to be.' Wrong. In fact there has never been a moment in my long and chequered career in which I have ever borne the remotest resemblance to Kenneth Cracknell, Esq.; but let that pass also. 'Your old enemy the Mad Bull is now a senior Old Bailey Judge.' As I read this the Florida sun seemed warmer and more delightful, the grass on the neat front lawns under the rainbow-hued sprinklers greener and more pleasant. 'Now what I want to ask your advice about, Rumpole, is this.' I turned another page; the round, schoolgirlish hand served to make the letter more bulky. 'Ken's got a murder and it's his first and naturally he wants to win, so I feel it's up to us to give him all the help we can. It all happened at Notting Hill Gate tube station (see the enclosed cuttings from *The Times* and the *News of the World* which will give you all the gen). But where you come in is with your marvellous expertise on questions of blood. It seems the client wrote a gruesome sort of letter, probably to the Devil or something equally creepy, in the victim's blood. What we want to know is, is this possible? I mean, wouldn't it congeal or something? And have you ever had a case of blood stains on paper? I don't really want Ken to know that I've asked your advice as he's awfully proud and touchy (like all radical barristers, I suppose) and really wants to feel that he's done it all himself. Claude is really quite well and very proud of Tristan.' Who the hell was Tristan, I wondered? 'As you say, he'll soon be old enough to sit up and draft an affidavit. Tristan, I mean.' Oh, of course, Tristan. The son and heir the Erskine-Browns conceived after one of their nights out at Covent Garden. 'At the moment we've got a most alarming Icelandic au pair and I have to keep out of her way in case she gives in her notice ...'

'Rumpole!' Hilda was calling to me from the other side of the lawn sprinkler as I stood by the postbox on the road at the end of the garden and read this letter which seemed to smell, even as I held it, comfortingly of fog and damp and old law reports and breakfast in Rex's Café. 'Is there anything in the post?'

'Do write if you can think of any sort of a cunning wheeze for Ken. Hope you're enjoying the sunshine. I do envy you. Phillida (Trant as was) Erskine-Brown.'

'No, nothing really. Just a postcard from my old clerk.' I stuffed Miss Trant's letter into my pocket; for some reason I felt guilty about it, as though I were already plotting the desperate course I was about to take.

'Henry's not wanting you back, is he?' Hilda asked suspiciously about my clerk, at which moment Erica emerged from the house with an ethnic shopping-basket and saw me smiling through the mist of the sprinkler.

'You look much happier today, Dad.'

'Yes. Henry doesn't want me back. There's no mention of that,' I told Hilda more or less truthfully.

'Oh well.' Hilda seemed relieved. 'We're just going down to the drug store.'

'What's the matter? Feeling seedy?'

'Don't be ridiculous, Rumpole. We're going to get Erica's cigarettes.'

As they went off chattering together to Erica's parked station-wagon, I began to wonder at the fact that Hilda, at her time of life, was starting to learn American.

The Importance of Blood Stains in Forensic Evidence by

Professor Andrew Ackerman, M.R.C.P., F.C.Path. The advantage of having a son who has done well in an academic career is that you can have your favourite books about you, even in Miami.

I was in the long, pleasantly cool room of the University library; around me blonde and bronzed young people, dressed in jeans and T-shirts, chewed gum and read the letters of Henry James, or some twelve-volume commentary on the works of Trollope. I leafed rapidly through Ackerman's familiar index. 'Blood stains on clothing ... On floors ... On ... On innocent bystanders ...' At first I couldn't believe that the Great Ackerman hadn't dealt with the problem, but then I became aware of the fact that Ken Cracknell's murder had, apparently, broken ground untrodden even by the Great Prince of the Mortuaries himself.

> So felt I like some watcher of the skies
> When a new planet swam into his ken ...

Or a new blood stain I told myself with delight, and I was clutching Andrew Ackerman's weighty volume and crossing the pleasant, tree-lined campus, threading my way among the bicycling and courting couples, when I came up to those former barbecue guests, Professor Blowfield of the Law Department and Paul Gilpin from English, together with that distinguished academic, young Nicholas Rumpole, Head of the Department of Sociology.

'It's the damnedest thing about Tiffany,' Paul was saying as I came up to them. 'She just vanished.'

'Vanished?' Professor Blowfield was saying. 'She can't have *vanished*. Why, here you are, Mr Rumpole. It seems we have a mystery on our hands.'

'Mystery? What mystery?' Fate seemed to have been unusually kind in the matter of handing out mysteries that day.

'Tiffany Jones never showed up at the Department,' Nick said. 'Yet Paul says she left home same time as usual.'

'And there's a young guy on the campus says Tiffany sold him her car yesterday. He picked it up from the street outside our apartment block – with the key on the offside wheel. How the hell's she going to go on living in Miami without a car?'

'She didn't say anything?' Professor Blowfield asked.

'Not that I can remember.'

I spent only a moment lamenting Paul Gilpin's loss of the handsome Tiffany; she had in any event seemed, as far as I clearly remembered, far too good for him, and then I approached Nick with the first stirrings of my Great Plan in mind.

'Nick. I must talk to you.'

'You remember Tiffany Jones, don't you, Dad? The economic statistician. She came to the barbecue.'

'Of course I remember her; but do statisticians ever disappear?'

'She'll call up, I guess. It can't *be* anything.' But Paul Gilpin didn't sound convinced.

'Perhaps she just melted away in the sunshine. Look, Nick. I'll take you out to lunch. Not the canteen. I don't think I could take another three-storey sandwich with a gherkin on a toothpick. Is there a quiet little chop-house somewhere? Where we could talk quietly?'

Chapter Six

We settled on the Magic Bamboo, a Chinese restaurant just off the campus. Clever little people, the Chinese, who would have made splendid Battle of Britain pilots, because they must be expert at seeing in the dark. The room, painted in black lacquer and gold, was plunged into a midnight gloom in which husbands no doubt lunched with their secretaries or other people's wives, or went on what might have been aptly known as blind dates. Faint lights dotted the tables with the effulgence of glow-worms, and pretty young Chinese waitresses passed among them with table-heaters and bowls of oriental delicacies.

'I've got to talk to you seriously, Nick,' I began, and wondered when I had talked to him seriously before.

'Look. If it's about money, there's absolutely no hurry. I know you'll make a contribution when you sell the flat.'

'It's not about money, Nick. Anyway, I may not sell the flat. I've got an idea I may need a pied-à-terre in Froxbury Mansions ...'

'What are you up to, Dad?' Nick looked at me with some suspicion, and I decided to approach my goal by a circuitous route.

'Look, Nick,' I said. 'When you were a boy, we used to have an oath of secrecy. Remember? If I found you reading comics under the bedclothes or eating gobstoppers? Your mother thought there was something lower class about a gobstopper ... Anyway, if I discovered any crime of that nature, the motto was N. A. W. T. S. W. M. B. O.'

'What on earth did that mean?' The young have short memories and Nick looked puzzled.

'Not A Word To She Who Must Be Obeyed,' I translated. 'So you see, if I planned to do the vanishing trick ... like what's her name, the disappearing statistician? Miss Tiffany Jones?'

'Dad. *Is* it about money?' Nick still looked vaguely anxious.

'No, dear boy. My dear Nick,' I set his mind at rest, 'it's about blood.'

'Blood?' Nick seemed not at all reassured.

'Listen, Nick. When I left England, I decided to plonk all my cards face down on the table. When I finally gave match point to His Honour Judge Bullingham and hung up my wig, I thought there were elements in my Chambers, deviously backed by our middle-of-the-road Q.C., M.P. Head of Chambers, who were quite pleased to see the back of old Rumpole. If I'm not mistaken, a certain sigh of relief went up from the clerk's room, where they prefer a barrister who's prepared to kiss his instructing solicitor's backside! But it now seems perfectly clear, Nick. They want me back. They can't do without me!'

'Dad ...' Nick was attempting some sort of interruption, but I was now in full flow.

'I've had a letter from Miss Phillida Trant, a girl whom I brought up in the law. She has written to me by airmail, Nick, sparing no expense. It seems they've got a murder which raises several nice questions of blood. So the cry has gone up from Equity Court in the Temple: Send for Rumpole!'

'Dad, you're not thinking of going back?'

It was a direct question and I decided to put off answering it by swigging the red wine the Chinese waitress had thoughtfully delivered. 'What's this? More Californian claret? Château Deadwood Stage? Not bad, Nick. Not bad at all. Better than Pommeroy's plonk, which in a bad year, if you remember, tasted as if they'd been treading toadstools and paddling in disinfectant.'

'Look. If Erica and I haven't shown we want you ...' Nick was not to be diverted.

'Bless you, Nick,' I hastily reassured him. 'Of course you have! I remember when you were a boy, quite a young boy, you were always about the place. We used to go for walks on Hampstead Heath. We used to track Indian spoor and swear to be blood-brothers. You recall that, don't you, Nick?'

'I don't think so.' For some reason those moments of past, childish excitement seemed to have slipped his memory.

'Well, that's what happened.' I had no doubt about it. 'And then you went off to school and university and forgot about me. I had to let you go and after a while, well, it's quite true, I hardly missed you. You'll have to let me go now, Nick. It won't be a great deprivation.'

It seemed to take a while for him to catch my drift, and when he did he looked puzzled, but not as appalled as a fond father might have hoped. 'I thought,' my son said slowly, 'Erica thought this too, that now we could really get to know one another.'

This did seem to me unnecessary. I mean, when you've seen a man through nappies and paid his school fees, you've really got past the formal introduction stage. 'We knew each other, Nick,' I reminded him. 'You knew me when I sat on the edge of the bath and told you about my murder cases. You don't want to know an old man dying of boredom in the sunshine.'

At which point a waitress passed with a tray loaded with small, steaming, cylindrical, white objects. With the aid of a pair of tongs she deposited one of these on each of our side plates.

'What are you planning?' Nick looked at me with deepening suspicion.

I took another swig of Château Cherokee or whatever it was and told him, 'Going home, Nick. Returning to base. Travel, you see, narrows the mind extraordinarily.' Then I gave him some lines of Ben Jonson that seemed to sum the matter up. They are displayed in all their glory in old Arthur Quiller-Couch's edition of *The Oxford Book of English Verse*, a battered India paper volume which travels always in my suitcase.

'No, I do know that I was born
To age, misfortune, sickness, grief:
But I will bear these with that scorn
As shall not need thy false relief.

Nor for my peace will I go far,
As wanderers do, that still do roam;
But make my strengths, such as they are,
Here in my bosom, and at home.'

'Good!' I peered through the blackout at the steaming shape on my side plate. 'They've brought us something to eat at last. I rather like Egg Rolls.' And before Nick could intervene I had seized the imagined delicacy and suddenly filled my mouth with what tasted like a mixture of warm scented soap and cotton fibres. The American passion for hygiene and dark restaurants had made me start my luncheon with an hors d'oeuvre of hot face-towel.

However, I give myself the credit of taking into full account the feelings of She Who Must Be Obeyed. I decided to leave her behind.

My wife Hilda had not, after all, throughout our long lives together, displayed any marked enthusiasm for the company of Rumpole. She frequently resented my presence, as well as my occasional absence at the end of the day in Pommeroy's Wine Bar. She took exception to my old anecdotes and criticized my hat. Hilda, I decided entirely with her best interests at heart, would be far happier if she stayed in America with Nick, Erica and the forthcoming infant Rumpole. I decided, I think wisely, on the selfless course of 'going it alone' as a result of an *ex parte* motion and without notice to the other side. In fact I saw no possible point in an argument with She; her natural desire to win it might force her to come with me, a course which I was convinced was not in the best interests of either of us.

So, with a growing sense of excitement and liberation, I laid my plans. I took time off from our hours at the beach to make a solitary visit to the headquarters of Gaelic Airlines, and secured a seat home in the steerage. As the great day approached I ordered a yellow taxi to call at the house at dawn, with a strict injunction against any sort of toot. When I left She's bedroom she moved uneasily in her sleep and muttered, 'Rumpole.' I was standing with my shoes in one hand and a packed suitcase in the other. I whispered, 'So long, Hilda' with all the cheerfulness of a schoolboy setting out to bicycle to the seaside on the first day of the summer holidays.

Hours later I was hanging in mid air somewhere over the Atlantic and a stewardess was handing me a miniature bottle of rum with the aloof distaste of a girl who felt her rightful place was with the champagne passengers behind the First Class curtain. I knew how dear old Tolstoy felt when he decided, late in life, to give the joys of matrimony the slip and set out for the railway station. I raised my plastic glass to the memory of the old Russian darling: it's never too late, after all, to strike a blow for freedom.

The machine owned by Gaelic Airlines was a contraption which I suspected was kept together with chewing gum and harp strings. As this unconvincing craft shuddered across the world, the strapping wenches in green kilts slammed trays of inedible food in front of those passengers fortunate enough to have dropped into an uneasy doze, babies screamed and piped music relayed the 'Londonderry Air'. It was a journey no one would be anxious to repeat, having all the glamour of a trip down Charing Cross tube station in the rush hour with the added element of fear.

Why was it that I was so anxious to repeat the miserable experience of being trundled through the stratosphere by courtesy of Gaelic Airlines? Looking back on it I think I must have deceived myself. When I got Miss Trant's letter, it seemed to me that the dull sunshine world of my retirement was suddenly refilled with interest. I convinced myself that I was still needed, that in fact Chambers couldn't do without me. What right had I, I wondered that morning, to deny my undoubted talents and lifetime's experience of blood stains to the British legal system? What was I doing, I asked myself, boring myself to death among a lot of geriatrics and citrus fruits, when the London underground system was still capable of yielding such a fine vintage murder? After only a short while with these thoughts, I came to the clear conclusion that there was only one way for Rumpole to go: sitting on the beach queuing up for death was out; I would meet my end in the full flood of a final speech, and with my wig on.

A confused number of hours, or perhaps days, later Ken Cracknell, the radical lawyer, and his chief fan and most vocal supporter, Miss Phillida Trant, were wending their weary way back to Chambers from Pommeroy's Wine Bar, where they had been refreshing themselves after a hard day in their respective courts. Ever hopeful of prolonging such moments of pleasure and delight, Cracknell asked his companion if she'd join him for a hamburger.

'Not tonight.' Miss Trant was genuinely grateful.

'Why not?'

'Claude's getting a baby-sitter. We're going to the Festival Hall. I promise ...'

'What?'

'I'll turn you over in my mind, during the Verdi *Requiem*,' Miss Trant smiled at him.

'Oh, thanks very much.' Cracknell appeared to find the prospect less than satisfying.

'We'll meet tomorrow anyway,' Miss Trant comforted him. 'We're co-defending in that long firm fraud down the Bailey.'

Cracknell sighed and accepted the crumb of comfort. They had now reached the doorway of our Chambers in Equity Court. 'I suppose I'd better go up and get the brief.'

'I suppose you had.' Looking carefully about her and seeing no one, in the doorway of our Chambers (so she told me later over a confessional bottle of claret in Pommeroy's) Mrs Erskine-Brown, née Trant, kissed Ken Cracknell. It was a moderately lengthy kiss. Miss Trant at first closed her eyes, the better to savour the experience, but when she opened them she found herself looking up at the room occupied by the devoted Ken; and there she saw an unexpected sight.

'Ken,' she whispered, 'isn't that the window of your room?'

'Yes. Yes, of course it is.' Ken turned and looked up at what he now regarded as 'his' room. The light was on in the early evening and on the drawn blind could be seen the silhouette of a figure who has become, I flatter myself, pretty familiar around the Temple and the Courts of Law. It was the shape of a man not tall but comfortably built (Claude Erskine-Brown might say fat) wearing a bow tie and smoking a small cigar.

'Oh dear,' said Miss Phillida Trant, staring at the clearly inhabited window, 'what *have* I done? I only wrote him a letter!'

Chapter Seven

I had let myself into Chambers that evening with the key I had never abandoned, and had gone straight up, the clerk's room being empty, to the room which I still considered to be mine. There I at once noted several changes: in place of my old 'Spy' caricatures of forgotten judges, there were posters for the North London Law Centre, for a rock concert in aid of Amnesty International, and for *The Legal Ass*, a new satirical magazine produced by the Hornsey Group of young and radical articled clerks. The space suit and the great globular plastic helmet hung on the back of the door; there were copies both of *Time Out* and of some periodical apparently written in the Welsh language with photographs of old men in dust-sheets singing in the open air. On the mantelpiece there were briefs marked Mr K. Cracknell, and others bearing the inscription Mr Owen Glendour-Owen. Among these pending cases were the papers in R. *v*. Simpson, Cracknell's first murder.

I went over to my old desk. It was covered with an assortment of papers, some unwashed coffee cups with cigarette ends and, in one case, half a ginger biscuit, soaking in the saucers. The eye was immediately assaulted by some luridly covered copies of a magazine entitled *Schoolgirl Capers* in which the schoolgirls in question, none of whom could have been a day under thirty-five, were wearing pigtails and abbreviated gym-slips and getting up to no sort of good whatsoever. I lit a small cigar, undid the tape which secured the brief in the Simpson murder and was standing by the window reading contentedly (delightedly conscious of the fact that there was no She Who Must Be Obeyed at home, awaiting my return) when the door burst open and a dark-browed and fiercely scowling young man appeared to make me instantly unwelcome.

'What on earth ...' the young man started, but I interrupted him.

'I don't think we've met, have we?'

'No, we haven't. I'm Ken Cracknell.'

Of course I should have remembered Miss Trant's letter giving me the low-down on our new 'radical' barrister. I don't know how it was that it slipped my memory, and I was tactless enough to say, 'You're new in the clerk's room, aren't you, Ken? I hope Henry hasn't been caught with his fingers in the coffee money. Oh, by the way, I'm Horace Rumpole.'

'I'm not a clerk!' For an egalitarian barrister with no side Cracknell seemed immoderately outraged. 'I'm a member of the Bar. I was a squatter.'

'Well, I hope you're not going to squat in here.' I looked round my old room, fearful of an invasion of my privacy.

'I was a squatter until they knew you were retiring for good,' Cracknell told me. 'Then they gave me a place in Chambers. Your place, Rumpole. I share this room with Owen Glendour-Owen.'

'They gave you my place?' I couldn't believe it. 'Who gave you my place?'

'The Head of Chambers. It's a squeeze in here for two. We certainly couldn't manage a third.'

'Guthrie Featherstone, Q.C., M.P., gave you my place!' I knew then how Julius Caesar felt when he saw his learned friend Brutus whip out the knife.

'With the full support of a Chambers meeting,' Cracknell added, bringing in the full cast of conspirators. 'That's my brief you're covering with your cigar ash. R. *v*. Simpson. It's a murder.'

'A case where, I gather from Miss Phillida Trant, you are a little out of your depth? I came over to see if I couldn't help out a little, on the question of blood.'

'Thank you.' Cracknell didn't sound particularly grateful. 'It's my first murder, and I intend to cope with it on my own.'

They were brave words, as even I had to recognize. I moved to young Cracknell and gave him an encouraging clap on the

shoulder, at which he flinched visibly. 'That's the spirit, Ken!
That's the spirit in which I took on the Penge Bungalow
Murders. Of course, in that case I'd also worked out my own
line of defence. What's yours?'

When I put the question, he looked at me with continued
and blank hostility. The truth of the matter, of course, was
that he hadn't worked out a defence at all. I didn't mean to
take immediate advantage of this weakness.

'We'll talk about it in the morning, shall we?' I said. 'Two
heads are always better than one.' Then I picked up one of the
magazines devoted to elderly schoolgirls. 'Oh, I'd be obliged if
you'd keep your private reading matter at home. I get some
rather sensitive criminals in here for conferences. Safe-blowers
are great supporters of Mrs Whitehouse. I must try not to
shock them.'

'That's not my private reading matter!' Cracknell appeared
to be making an effort to speak and suppressing considerable
rage. 'Those are exhibits in an obscene publications case I've
got up in the north of England. Grimble Crown Court, as it
so happens.'

I put on my hat to leave him then, but I didn't go before I
had congratulated him on an excellent start at the Bar. 'Obscenity. Murder. You're leading an exciting life, aren't you, Ken?
For one so young.' I moved to the door and smiled. 'I'll speak
to our Head of Chambers about you in the morning. See if
he can't fix up a little annexe for you somewhere.' And before
young Cracknell could explode I was off to savour the pleasures
of a solitary evening at Froxbury Mansions, many miles away
from She Who Must Be Obeyed.

The next morning, when I presented myself in the clerk's
room, my appearance produced what I can only describe as a
stunned and embarrassed silence. It was not until I had gone
upstairs to announce the glad news of my return to our
learned Head of Chambers, Guthrie Featherstone, Q.C., M.P.,
that Henry recovered himself sufficiently to speak to the as-
sembled company of Miss Trant, Ken Cracknell, Dianne and
Uncle Tom.

'I can't believe it!' Henry sounded, according to Miss

Trant, as though he'd just witnessed some sort of rising from the dead.

'If he's back already, I don't know why he ever left.' Dianne made her puzzled contribution.

'He left because he lost ten cases in a row before Judge Bullingham. He got terribly depressed about it,' Miss Trant explained to them. 'Oh dear. I only wrote him a letter.' She looked round at their solemn faces and added, as a cheerful afterthought, 'Probably just a visit. He won't be staying long.'

'I gave you good warning.' Uncle Tom nodded wisely. 'He'll always be bobbing back like a bloody opera singer, making his "positively last appearance".'

'Mr Featherstone wants to see him. He'll sort it out, I'm sure.' Henry shelved the problem of Rumpole and then leafed through his diary to check on the future plans of the rest of his stable of hacks and thoroughbreds. He asked Cracknell how long he gave the long firm fraud he was starting that morning, working in double harness with Miss Phillida Trant.

'At least four weeks,' Cracknell said with satisfaction, and Miss Trant nodded; she was also thinking of the fine pile of refreshers.

Henry shook his head doubtfully. 'I'm afraid it's going to clash with your obscenity up north,' he said. 'We'll have to return the brief. And then there's the murder coming up.'

'You'll be getting awfully rich for a radical barrister.' Miss Trant smiled at Cracknell in a proud and almost proprietorial way.

'I can't leave the fraud, Henry.' Ken Cracknell was clear where his duty lay. 'So I may have to give up the dirty books. Come on, Phillida. Time we got down to the Bailey.'

As the growing friendship between Phillida and Ken led them down Fleet Street together, towards the shining dome of the Edwardian *Palais de Justice* and the joint defence of a couple of over-optimistic second-hand car salesmen, I was closeted with our Head of Chambers who rose, on my arrival, with the air of a somewhat more heroic Macbeth who is forcing himself to invite Banquo's ghost to take a seat, and would he care for a cigarette.

'Horace! My dear old Horace. How good of you to look us

up while you're in England. We've all missed you terribly. As everyone says, "Chambers just isn't Chambers without old Horace Rumpole."'

'*Is* that what they say?' Personally I had some doubts about it.

'And you look so well!' Featherstone went on, I thought over-eagerly. 'So remarkably well! I've never seen you looking better. Hilda enjoying it out there, is she? I'm sure she is.'

'She Who Must Be Obeyed is perfectly contented. She was never particularly interested in blood.' I sat down and lit a small cigar, apparently to Featherstone's disappointment.

'I'm not quite with you, Horace?'

'I've had quite enough of compassionate leave, Featherstone. I've decided to come back and fight it out down the Old Bailey.'

'Horace,' Featherstone gulped like a man fighting for breath. 'Is that really wise? You were getting dreadfully tired, as I remember.'

I blew out smoke and gave him a sample of Ben Jonson's 'Farewell to the World'.

> 'Nor for my peace will I go far,
> As wanderers do, that still do roam;
> But make my strengths, such as they are,
> Here in my bosom, and at home.'

I wandered to the window and looked out at the green grass, the last damp autumn roses and the familiar grey clouds. 'This is my home, Featherstone. These Chambers have been my home for over forty years. And, as you so eloquently put it, "Chambers just isn't Chambers without old Horace Rumpole."'

'Rumpole ...' Featherstone, to my annoyance, was doing his best to interrupt my flow.

'I'm glad you said that, Featherstone! Up to now I haven't noticed the red carpet, or the cut flowers on my desk with the compliments of the management. When I put my nose into the clerk's room this morning, they failed to uncork the Moët and Chandon. The champagne was flowing like cement!'

'Well. The fact is ...' Featherstone tried to sound confidential. 'You see, Rumpole, your coming back would rather rock the boat of Chambers.'

I wasn't sure I liked the drift of his argument. 'It would?' I said. 'What do you mean, it *would*? I *am* back!'

Featherstone cleared his throat, I'm glad to say in some embarrassment. 'Since your departure we've taken on two new members. We reckoned you were worth at least two other barristers, so we've put two in your room. Glendour-Owen has joined us from Cardiff, and young Ken Cracknell ...'

'I've met Cracknell,' I assured him. 'He's got himself a nice little murder. I might just be able to help him.'

'Ken's got your room, Rumpole.' Featherstone was becoming more determined, no doubt in desperation.

'My room? Oh yes, I saw him hanging about in my room. Quite welcome, I'm sure. Provided he doesn't litter the place with licentious comics.'

Featherstone went over to the defensive. 'Well, how were we to know you were coming back? It's a *fait accompli*. We've given Ken a seat. And Glendour-Owen, who has a huge practice in motor insurance. "Knock-for-Knock" Owen they call him on the Welsh circuit. We've promised them both seats.'

'Can't you find them seats in some convenient passage?' I didn't see the difficulty.

'We've promised them a *room*.' Featherstone looked pained.

'Then rent some more accommodation. Think big, Featherstone! Expand!'

'We can't afford that, Horace.' Now he looked particularly gloomy. 'We've all got to cut back, reduce our cash flow. England's in for four hard years.'

'Is there no mitigation?' Featherstone said nothing and I gave him a long, accusing look, which I was pleased to see made him squirm visibly. Then I spoke more in sorrow than in anger. 'Are you trying to tell me, Featherstone, in your devious and political kind of way, that there is no room for Rumpole at the Inn?'

'I'm afraid, Horace, that is exactly it!' Featherstone's gloom was impenetrable.

I took a long pause and then said cheerfully, 'I know exactly what I shall do.'

'Go back to Florida?' The good Guthrie seemed to see a glimpse of light at the end of the tunnel. 'Of course you should. I'm sure we all envy you the sunshine, and wish you many long and happy years in your retirement.'

But I interrupted him in a way that clearly dashed his fragile hopes. 'Go back to Florida? Certainly not. I'm going to give up being an orange.' I moved to the door, and then turned back to smile at Featherstone. 'I shall squat.'

Chapter Eight

It was all very well. I had made my position clear. I was a squatter, and I intended to squat; but as I contemplated empty days ahead, stuck with the *Times* crossword and always in the way, I have to confess that the first fine burst of excitement which had sent me winging over the Atlantic on the Gaelic contraption began to dry to a mere dribble. How foolish should I begin to feel after three weeks of squatting with no work; and should I finally be forced back to the Sunshine State, and She Who Must Be Obeyed, with my tail between my legs? There was nothing I could do about it, of course, except to push open the door of the clerk's room and make it clear that Rumpole was himself again, and available for contested breathalyzers. I comforted myself once more with Ben Jonson.

'But what we are born for we must bear:
Our frail condition it is such
That what to all may happen here,
If't chance to me, I must not grutch.

Else I my state should much mistake
To harbour a divided thought
From all my kind: that for my sake
There should a miracle be wrought.'

And then a miracle, of a sort, happened. As I pushed open the door of the clerk's room, Henry was on the telephone, and as I loitered, lighting a small cigar, I distinctly heard him say, 'Is that Grimble 43021? Austin, Swink and Pardoner? Oh, could I speak to Mr Handyside please?'

Henry was on the phone to Albert Handyside. Albert had been my old clerk, but had left us after what I felt to be a quite unnecessary inquiry into his management of the petty cash by that infernal busybody Claude Erskine-Brown. Albert had then crossed the Great Divide and gone to work as a solicitor's clerk in a grey and wind-blasted town called Grimble, in the north of England. It was from his firm there that Albert had sent me that unusual little murder in which I had defended the leading lady of the Grimble Rep. with a result which was certainly in her interest, if not in the interest of justice; and I knew that, all else being equal, Albert Handyside might have a leading part to play in the resurrection of Rumpole's practice.

'Oh, Albert.' Henry had got through to his great predecessor whom he was addressing in a somewhat patronizing manner. 'This is Henry. Yes, old boy, Henry. Mr Cracknell's clerk. It's about our obscenity up north, in your neck of the woods. I'm afraid Mr Cracknell's tied up at the Old Bailey for the next two weeks. Miss Trant's in the case with him. Mr Glendour-Owen? He's doing a long rape in Swansea. I'm terribly sorry I can't oblige you. There just isn't anyone in Chambers.'

No one in Chambers! I can only suppose that Henry wasn't aware of the familiar figure standing behind him, smoking a small cigar and ready to fulfil any mission however daring or distant, even in the Grimble Crown Court.

'Henry,' I said loudly, and when he didn't move increased the decibels with, 'A moment of your valuable time, Henry.'

'Yes, Mr Rumpole. What is it?' Henry said testily as he covered the mouthpiece with his hand. 'I'm just on the telephone.'

'On the telephone to old Albert Handyside? Who used to be my head clerk when you didn't know Bloomsbury County Court from London Sessions,' I reminded him. 'Put him through to me, will you, Henry. I'd be glad of a word or two with old Albert. I'll be upstairs,' and I made for the door so that I could speak in private to my old clerk.

'You'll be in Mr Cracknell's room?' Henry asked, and I put him right, quite firmly.

'No, Henry. I'll be in *my* room.'

'Mr Rumpole! Good to hear your voice, sir. I thought you'd retired.'

'Good to hear *your* voice, Albert. Retired? No. Whatever

54

gave you that idea? I just popped over to the States, you know. My wife's gone out there to be with young Nick and his family. But I'm back now, foot-loose, fancy-free and ready for any crime you care to mention.'

'Well, Mr Rumpole. I don't know ...'

'And I'm delighted,' I cut him off before he could become even more doubtful, 'really delighted we're doing this little obscenity case together in the north of England. Have a bit of fun. Quite like old times, eh, Albert?'

'You're doing it, Mr Rumpole?' Albert sounded puzzled, and not quite as overjoyed as I'd anticipated.

'Oh yes. Didn't Henry tell you? I expect it slipped his mind. You see, there's no one else to do it. Ken Cracknell's so terribly busy these days.'

'Perhaps I'd better have a word with your clerk again, sir. I'd be glad to have you up here again.'

'Yes, of course. I'll put you back to Henry. I'm snowed under with work, of course, quite snowed under.' I looked round at the briefs marked Glendour-Owen and K. Cracknell, not one bearing the welcome name of Rumpole. 'But I'll manage to squeeze your little obscenity in. Look forward to it. Give my love to Grimble.'

I then jiggled the instrument and when I heard Henry's distracted voice I told him that Albert Handyside wanted a word with him, and that it was all quite like old times. Then I replaced the receiver and relaxed with a sense of something accomplished, something done.

As I sat back in my old chair (creaking, swivelling and leaking stuffing), I glanced across at that magnet which had drawn me across the Atlantic, the brief in R. v. Simpson, the Notting Hill Gate underground stabbing, labelled, by some oversight of fate, Mr K. Cracknell. I heaved myself to my feet, went over to it and slid off the tape.

The first thing I saw was a coloured photostat of the sheet of paper with the letters said to have been scrawled in the victim's blood. The blood itself would no doubt provide infinite opportunities for speculation and debate, and it was the problem of the blood on which I had first been consulted by Miss Phillida Trant. What interested me now was the message. It was the first time I had read it; it was short but somewhat obscure, scrawled but possible to read, and it ran: SUNLIGHT TO CHILDREN OF SUN, BLOOD TO CHILDREN OF DARK.

Well now I realized why fate and Gaelic Airlines and Miss Trant's letter had all combined to bring me winging back to England. I was the only member of Chambers with a chance of helping the unfortunate Simpson. I had the knowledge, and I must be careful how I handled it in acquiring my next Notable British Trial.

'Isn't that Cracknell's brief?'

I turned to find the room inhabited by a small, smiling, grey-haired Celt in a black jacket and pinstripes.

You must be Glendour-Owen by the sound of you, I speculated as the intruder put his briefcase down on *my* desk and started to pollute the area with a number of briefs in trumpery running-down cases. I decided to avoid any immediate confrontation.

'Well, of course you're welcome, Glendour-Jones.'

'Owen.'

'Well, of course you're welcome, Owen. Any time. If you can find yourself a corner. Be a bit of a squash, I'm afraid, until we get things sorted out.'

'Rumpole ...' The Welsh wizard of the car insurance racket seemed about to protest, but he was interrupted by a knock and the entrance of Henry carrying a brief. It was in the Grimble Crown Court, entitled R. *v.* Meacher, and on it I was satisfied to see that the name 'Cracknell' had been struck out and 'Rumpole' substituted.

'It seems Mr Handyside wants to instruct you in this obscenity, sir,' said Henry, with no particular enthusiasm. 'Mr Cracknell being in a difficulty.'

'Does he really?' I thought it best to affect complete surprise. 'Oh well, I'll do my best to fit it in. I don't mind doing returned briefs, just until things get going again, Henry.' At which point I reached out and grabbed the brief firmly before there was any chance of Henry changing his mind.

'Things, Mr Rumpole?' said Henry looking at me, as I thought, coolly.

'My practice, Henry. Solicitors have been asking for me,

56

have they?' I was undoing the brief, and saw the now familiar covers of *Schoolgirl Capers*.

'No, sir. Not exactly.' Henry spoke without mercy. 'The word seems to have got around, about you losing all those cases down the Bailey.'

'A long run of Judge Bullingham, Glendour-Owen,' I explained my ill fortune to the newcomer. 'That's not going to happen again.'

'How long will you be staying this time, sir?' Henry asked, and the Welshman's little eyes were fixed on me as he chipped in with, 'Yes, Rumpole. How long will you be staying?'

I considered the matter, and gave them the best answer I could. 'Well, I don't know exactly. Nothing wrong with my ticker, thank God, and a good intake of claret keeps me astonishingly regular. I suppose I might be here for another ten, fifteen years.'

At which neither of them looked particularly delighted, and Henry went with a sniff of disapproval. 'Gentlemen in Chambers getting their own work, Mr Rumpole,' he said. 'It's not in the best traditions of the Bar.'

As the door closed I saw the Welsh invader make a beeline for *my* chair. I made a quick dash round the corner of the desk and had got my bottom firmly in it before he could hitch up his trousers. Then I made my comment on our cool clerk. ' "Best traditions of the Bar"! He sounds like Judge Bullingham.'

'Rumpole.' The Welshman seemed to be taking in breath for some prolonged protest. As I was in no mood for a lengthy address, I decided that a soft answer would turn away wrath, and that it might be just possible to set this bumptious little person, who was clearly one of nature's Circus Judges, on a road to promotion, which might keep him from hurling himself at my chair every time I felt the need to sit down. Accordingly I looked at him with warmth and admiration.

'Glendour-Owen. You're not *the* Glendour-Owen, are you? Not the one who does all the car insurance?'

'Well, yes. "Knock-for-Knock" Owen is what they call me – on the South Wales Circuit.' He smiled immodestly.

'I was a guest at the Sheridan Club last night,' I lied, I

57

hoped in a good cause. 'The Lord Chancellor was talking about you.'

'The Lord Chancellor?' He breathed the words like a sort of prayer. He was clearly ripe for the Circus.

'"That 'Knock-for-Knock' Owen who does a lot of motor insurance," the Lord Chancellor was saying, "would make a wonderful Circuit Judge. Just the type we need in Wales." He couldn't speak too highly ...'

'A Judge? I've never even considered ...' Now the ambitious Celt was lying.

I gave him a beam of encouragement. 'Consider it, Owen. Turn it over in your mind, as you sit in the tube on the way to Uxbridge County Court. The Lord Chancellor's got his eye on you!' I opened my new brief in the obscene publications case and spread it liberally about the surface of the desk, dismissing the embryo Judge with a wave of the small cigar. 'Now, if you don't mind, I've got a practice to look after.'

Chapter Nine

'The expense of spirit in a waste of shame
Is lust in action; and till action, lust
Is perjured, murd'rous, bloody, full of blame,
Savage, extreme, rude, cruel, not to trust;
Enjoyed no sooner but despisèd straight;
Past reason hunted; and no sooner had,
Past reason hated, as a swallowed bait,
On purpose laid to make the taker mad ...'

I was reciting to myself *con brio* the words of Shakespeare's
most embittered sonnet as some sort of entertainment to keep
me going during the reading of *Schoolgirl Capers* Vol. 1,
numbers 1 to 6, which it was my tiresome duty to go through
before enjoying the treat of an obscenity trial at the Grimble
Crown Court. I also had to read two remarkably dull works
of fiction entitled *Double Dating in the Tower of Terror* and
Manacle me, Darling, but I kept these back as the main stodge
and I was flicking through *Schoolgirl Capers* Vol. 1, number 4,
by way of an hors d'oeuvre, all the other items of suspect
material being in my briefcase which was open on the floor
beside me. Also open on the floor beside me, as I come to
remember it, was a half-full (you can tell that I was feeling
sufficiently comfortable and optimistic not to say half-empty)
bottle of Pommeroy's plonk, which I found left a more pleasant
afterglow than the perfectly acceptable Californian Château
Wells Fargo, or whatever it was that I had grown used to
drinking. I may say I was on my second bottle of Pommeroy's
Ordinary, and I was full out on the sofa, cushions under the
head, jacket and shoes off, and the open waistcoat deep in
the snow of cigar ash. A saucer of small cigar ends was also
on the floor beside me; in the kitchen, relics of my various
meals (I went in for a regular diet of boiled eggs and toast, I

don't aspire to *haute cuisine*) covered the table and comfortably filled the sink; among my many talents (blood, typewriters and the art of cross-examination) I do not include bed-making, so the bedroom had what might be charitably described as a 'lived-in' appearance.

Before my eyes the middle-aged schoolgirls capered, lifting their tunics, sticking out their tongues and gyrating in a lethargic, half-gymnastic sort of way, which I found singularly asexual. I turned the page and recited the sonnet to them.

> 'Mad in pursuit, and in possession so;
> Had, having, and in quest to have, extreme;
> A bliss in proof, and proved, a very woe;
> Before, a joy proposed; behind, a dream ...'

Had I not known it to be impossible, I might have thought I heard the sound of a key in the front door of the mansion flat. I went on reciting.

> 'All this world well knows; yet none knows well
> To shun the heaven that leads men to this hell.'

'Rumpole!'

But this was no dream. I distinctly heard the front door open and a clarion cry with which I was all too familiar. I sprang into activity; my long training in crime stood me in excellent stead, and I started to remove clues and reorganize the scene. The saucer of cigar ends was tipped into the wastepaper basket, the bottles and glass went on the window sill where they might be concealed by the curtain until I got up at dawn, I fastened my briefcase on the sexually explicit material and ...

'Rumpole! I know perfectly well you're there.' It was a familiar voice.

I looked round for incriminating signs and saw *Schoolgirl Capers* Vol. 1, number 4, on the sofa. It was the work of seconds by a determined man able to keep his head in an emergency to thrust it behind the sofa cushions. I then took in a deep breath, regretted I hadn't finished the second bottle of plonk for courage, and threw open the door that opened into our entrance hall or vestibule.

'What've you been doing, Rumpole? Trying to lie doggo?'

She Who Must Be Obeyed was standing there surrounded by suitcases. Hers, I knew with a sinking heart, was to be no fleeting visit.

After I had left America, it seemed there was a family gathering round the swimming bath. Nick was reading the *New York Review of Books*, Erica was listening to folk music on her cassette machine and knotting string to make hanging plant-pot holders, and Hilda was standing glowering into the water, drawing her cardigan about her as if cold.

'I shall never understand Rumpole, doing a bolt like that!' said She.

'We couldn't keep him here for ever.' Nick did his best to sound reasonable.

'Sneaking out by taxi in the middle of the night. I can't understand how he got back to England.' Hilda's voice, it seems, was full of anger and contempt.

'I think on a cheap standby with Gaelic Airlines.' Nick, of course, knew all about it.

'Back in the flat! We'll never get it sold with Rumpole in it!'

'He wanted you to stay here, you know.' My son Nick was appointed as my advocate.

'Stay here without Rumpole? I've never heard anything like it!' said Hilda, showing a hitherto unknown taste for the presence of Rumpole.

'He thought you'd be happier here.' Erica, give her her due, was doing her best to support Nick's side of the argument.

At this Hilda clicked her tongue, drew her faithful cardigan still more tightly about her and seemed troubled by a new and awful thought. 'You don't think,' she said to Nick, 'you don't think that possibly ... at his age!'

'What don't I think, Mum?'

After some sort of inner struggle my wife made herself say it. 'Another woman!'

'That's absolutely ridiculous!' Nick told me he laughed in a way which I didn't find altogether flattering.

'Is it?' She was extremely doubtful. 'Men get afflicted by a dreadful Indian summer or something. I'm always reading about it.'

'Not Dad. It's just his endless love affair with the Old Bailey.'

But my wife wouldn't have this. 'He's not in love with the Old Bailey. Judge Bullingham put him off the Old Bailey. It must be ... *something* else. And I know exactly what I shall do about it.'

'What're you going to do about it, Mum?' Erica was curious.

'You'll see. I shall ...' For a moment Hilda seemed hesitant, then she said, 'I shall do my duty!' At which she buttoned up her cardigan and went into the house. Forty-eight hours later she was at Heathrow Airport, and so, like a wolf on the fold, she came down by taxi on Froxbury Mansions and shattered the peace of Rumpole.

'Well, Hilda. This is a surprise!' I did my best to smile, but she wasn't smiling.

Instead she asked, 'Why weren't you at the airport?'

'Well, I can't spend my evenings hanging about Heathrow in the vague hope that you'll descend from the skies.' It seemed a reasonable explanation, but it was clearly unacceptable to Hilda.

'I sent you a telegram.'

'You didn't.'

'Of course I did.'

By this time we were both in our living-room and I was eyeing the waste-paper basket with a certain amount of guilt. 'If it had a typed envelope ...'

'Most telegrams do.'

I picked up the waste-paper basket and found, among ash to equal the destruction of Pompeii, a large number of old cigar butts, a handful of unopened bills and communications from the Inland Revenue (opening such things, I have found, merely causes headaches and other nervous disorders) and an unopened cablegram.

'I must have mistaken it for another *billet doux* from the tax-gatherers,' I said by way of explanation.

At which She made her usual clicking sound and looked desperately round Casa Rumpole. 'It looks like a rubbish tip in here, Rumpole. I suppose the washing-up hasn't been done for a week. And I saw that the "For Sale" sign has been taken down.'

'Well, I could hardly have some ... some bright young man in the media move in with his extended family. Not while I'm living here, Hilda.' I thought the explanation quite adequate, but her next question took me by surprise.

'Why are you living here, Rumpole?'

'It's ... it's my home.' It was the best I could do, but meant honestly. However, She Who Must Be Obeyed picked holes in my reply.

'*Our* home was in America, Rumpole,' she said. 'We were perfectly happy. You'd retired and ...'

'*You* were perfectly happy,' I corrected her.

'Sneaking away like that! Doing a bolt! Leaving that ridiculous note telling me to stay behind and be happy!' She stared at me, the only word is 'implacably'.

'What's at the bottom of this, Rumpole?'

'What's at ... where?'

'What's at the bottom of your extraordinary behaviour? I shall find out. Don't think I shan't find out. You can't hide anything from me, Rumpole!'

For once I was at a loss for an answer. I shrugged vaguely, having not the faintest idea what she was on about. Then she decided to lift the pressure and rise for a short adjournment.

'In the meantime,' Hilda said, 'you can go and put the kettle on. I think I'll have a cup of instant.'

'She Who Must Be Obeyed,' I murmured as I went obediently to the kitchen door.

'And don't start washing up in there, Rumpole,' Hilda called after me. 'Leave it to me. You'll only break something!'

'I hear, O Master of the Blue Horizons,' I told myself as I went into the kitchen. I looked round the comforting mess and said goodbye to my last meal of boiled eggs and claret. Freedom – I suppose I should have known that it was too good to last.

Chapter Ten

The next day I was standing in front of the desk in what I had been forced to regard as the communal room in Chambers, sorting through the exhibits in my new obscenity case before having a conference with the client Meacher and old Albert Handyside from instructing solicitors in Grimble. As I shuffled through the exhibits I noticed the absence of one item, viz. *Schoolgirl Capers* Vol. 1, number 4. I also became aware of a tall and anxious figure who had percolated into the room. It was our learned Head of Chambers, Guthrie Featherstone, Q.C., M.P., and as I looked up at him I remembered that he might, for once in his distinguished career, come in useful to Rumpole.

'Featherstone,' I said in my most ingratiating manner, 'you play golf with old Keith from the Lord Chancellor's office. Put in a word for that Welsh chap who hangs about in this room.'

'Glendour-Owen?' Featherstone looked puzzled.

'That's the fellow,' I told him. 'He's longing to be a Circuit Judge. Eaten up with ambition for the post. Can't you do something for the poor devil? I mean, there must be vast, lawless stretches of Wales where he could make himself useful.' I was still searching among my papers. *Schoolgirl Capers* Vol. 1, numbers 3 and 5 all present and correct. Number 4 still gone missing. 'Look, Featherstone old darling. I'm just about to have a conference.'

Featherstone looked somewhat taken aback at the news and said, 'I hope this is a one-off, Rumpole.'

'What on earth's happened to *Schoolgirl Capers* number 4?' I demanded of no one in particular. I saw that Featherstone had moved somewhat closer to my deskful of adult reading, sniffing slightly as if he were a dog who had a whiff of a juicy joint cooking. But when he spoke, it was still in a voice full of sadness and disapproval.

'I mean, Henry told me you were taking on this case to help out Ken. I just hope you're not going to make a habit of it. You see, we just haven't got the accommodation.'

'Make a habit of it?' I looked at him, puzzled. 'I've been making a habit of it for the last forty years.'

The phone on the desk rang. It was Henry to say that old Albert Handyside and the client Meacher were awaiting my pleasure. I told him to shoot them up with all convenient speed. As he moved to the door Featherstone said, 'I'll talk to you later. Oh, and Rumpole . . .'

'I seem to have lost . . . half the evidence.' I was still searching, hopelessly, for the missing *Caper*.

Featherstone nerved himself to say, rather too casually, 'I happen to be sitting on the Parliamentary Committee on Pornography. I wonder if you'd let me have a glance at those magazines later? Purely as a public duty, of course.'

'Oh, purely as a public duty? How brave of you, Featherstone!'

The learned Head of Chambers took my tribute with a puzzled frown and vanished, to be quickly replaced by Mr Meacher, Pornographer-in-Chief to the town of Grimble, a large, red-faced man with a bright blue suit, suede shoes, a gold bracelet watch, a North-country accent and an overwhelming smell of after-shave, and Albert Handyside. And so the conference began. Rumpole was in business again.

At which moment the following disastrous event occurred on the home front. She Who Must Be Obeyed paused in the much-needed hoovering of our living-room to plump the sofa cushions. Under one of these cushions she discovered a strange, and to her eye, deeply disturbing object; that is to say, a much-thumbed copy of *Schoolgirl Capers* Vol. 1, number 4. She picked it up as though it were some unmentionable vermin that had crept into the warmth of our sofa and died and, holding it at arm's length, she leafed through the contents. She had got to page 45 when she realized that a desperate remedy was needed. She wrapped the awful exhibit in a sheet of plain brown paper, put on her hat and coat and went straight round to the surgery of our local G.P., a somewhat dour and anxious Scot named Doctor Angus MacClintock.

During the statutory thirty-three and a half minutes for which Hilda was kept sitting in the waiting-room she looked neither to right nor to left; and she read neither last year's *Illustrated London News* nor the June 1976 *Punch*. She held the horrible parcel tightly on her lap, as though it might wriggle in a sensual fashion and slither away. When her turn was called she went straight into the Doctor's consulting room without removing her hat.

'Mrs Rumpole.' Dr MacClintock rose anxiously to greet her. He was a grey man in a grey room and his voice was calculated to produce an instant awareness of death in the healthiest patient. 'I thought you were sunning yourself out in Florida. Nothing serious, I hope?'

'Yes, it is. Very serious.'

'What are the symptoms?'

To which she answered simply, 'The symptoms are Rumpole.'

'Oh dear.'

'I had to come, Doctor.' Hilda spoke in a voice of doom. 'Something terribly strange has happened to my husband.'

'Terribly strange? Oh dear me. Not his back again?'

'*Worse* than his back. I found this. He'd been reading *this*!'

At which Hilda stripped off the discreet brown-paper covering and revealed *Schoolgirl Capers* Vol. 1, number 4, in its full embarrassment to the Doctor's astonished gaze.

'I'm very much afraid, Dr MacClintock,' Hilda told him, 'that Rumpole has *got sex*.'

Meanwhile, up at the mill, I was slogging away and trying to earn an honest bob or two in conference with the bookseller, who was describing the difficulties which face an honest vendor of adult reading material in the town of Grimble. There was, it seemed, a local Savonarola or Calvin who was a particular thorn in Mr Meacher's flesh.

'This Alderman Launcelot Pertwee,' he told me, 'Chairman of the Watch Committee, member of the Festival of Light, President of the Clean-Up-Grimble Society, walks into my Sowerby Street shop when I'm out at golf.'

'Mr Meacher here owns the Adult Reading Mart with twenty

branches in the north of England.' My former clerk Albert Handyside provided the information. Twenty dubious book-shops sounded to me a veritable Eldorado, a promise of briefs beyond price.

'And my damn fool of an assistant, Dobbs,' Meacher went on, 'only sells Pertwee two hundred quid's worth of adult read-ing, films and visual aids. Of course, Peeping Pertwee's round to the Chief Constable with them in five minutes.'

It was then that I gave Meacher the value of my advice on his particular class of criminal trial. 'Mr Meacher,' I said. 'I have been thinking hard about the nature of your defence. I've read all the numbers of *Schoolgirl Capers* ... I seem to have lost Vol. 1, number 4 ... It doesn't matter.'

'Mr Rumpole'll have your defence well worked out, Mr Meacher.' Dear old Albert Handyside was always a great support to me.

'I'd like to go for Prying Pertwee.' Meacher was clearly longing for revenge. 'The man's a hypocrite. There's been some very nasty rumours about the Alderman.'

I lit a small cigar and returned my client to the realm of pure law. 'My first thought was that the prosecution's barking up the wrong tree. They should have done you under the Trade Descriptions Act.'

'What do you mean exactly, Mr Rumpole?' I could see poor old Albert looking puzzled. I did my best to explain.

'Adult reading material, Mr Meacher. Isn't it put forward as something likely to stimulate the senses, to send a young man's fancy wild with unsatisfied desire, to promote venery and to conjure up, for the lonely and unfulfilled citizens of Grimble, all the abandoned delights of the bedchamber?'

'Well, to be quite honest with you, Mr Rumpole,' Meacher admitted, 'yes.'

'Let's be *really* honest,' I replied. 'No! I have looked, swiftly I must confess, through this material. There is only one word for it. "Off-putting".'

'I'm not quite with you.' Meacher's expression was pained.

'I have been thinking to myself ...' I blew out smoke, enjoying the philosophical argument. 'What are the least aphrodisiac conceptions, the things most deadening to lust?

Income Tax? V.A.T.? String vests? Chest protectors? Cardigans? Woollen socks worn with sandals? Fish fingers? Party Political Broadcasts? As deterrents to the tender passion, I would say they all come a bad second to *Schoolgirl Capers* Vols. 1 to 6 and *Double Dating in the Tower of Terror*, and you can throw in *Manacle me, Darling* as an additional extra!'

'Mr Rumpole.' Meacher appeared to be about to protest; but I wasn't accepting questions yet.

'*Schoolgirl Capers!* There can't be a schoolgirl in there under forty!' I paused and relit the wilting cigar. 'However, attractive as it would be to point out that this material is merely a boring waste of money, I shan't in fact take that line.'

'I'm glad to hear it.' Mr Meacher looked distinctly relieved. 'This is a serious case, Mr Rumpole.'

'Yes, of course,' I agreed with him, 'far more serious than the tripe removed by Alderman Pertwee.'

'Stock valued at at least two hundred pounds,' Meacher protested, and I stood to give him what I still believe was one of my finest speeches in the law.

'Stock valued beyond gold, Mr Meacher! Our priceless liberties. Free speech, Mr Meacher! That's how we're going to win this one. The birthright of the Briton, to read and write just as the fancy takes him.' The time had come to call on Wordsworth and I gave Mr Meacher, for the price of his con., a few lines from the old darling.

> 'It is not to be thought of that the flood
> Of British Freedom, which, to the open sea
> Of the world's praise, from dark antiquity
> Hath flowed, with pomp of waters, unwithstood,
> Should perish!'

As I recited I paced, and as I passed the door it opened and there was Ken Cracknell, standing there eagerly, his arms full of papers and other tools of his trade. 'Some other time, Cracknell!' I hissed at him. 'Can't you see I've got a conference?'

'This is my room!' Cracknell sounded outraged.

'Some other time.' And I promised him, by way of compensation, 'I'll want to see you about that little murder of yours. I've had some ideas, as it so happens. Run along now.' At which

I shut the door on Cracknell and walked back to my desk, still addressing the North-country bookseller in ringing tones. 'Words, we shall tell the jury, Mr Meacher, must be free, for freedom is indivisible! Man has the right to read the boldest speculations, the most dazzling philosophy, to question God, to explore the universe, to follow poetry into the most exquisite sensuality or the finest religious ecstasy. So he must be granted the freedom to blunt his brains on *Schoolgirl Capers*. I utterly deplore the rubbish you are selling, but I'll defend to the death anyone's right to read it!' I concluded, giving him Voltaire, the Rumpole version.

There was a long pause. My oratory was having an effect; something was stirring in what remained of Mr Meacher's mind after a prolonged course of adult reading. 'Free speech, eh?' he said, blinking.

'In a nutshell,' I told him.

'I like it, Mr Rumpole.' A slow smile spread over Mr Meacher's florid features. 'I really like it. As a defence, I would say, it has a certain amount of class.'

A day or so later I was chewing a piece of breakfast toast and reading the daily paper when up spoke She Who Must Be Obeyed, whom I had noticed eyeing me curiously of late.

'What are you reading *now*, Rumpole?'

'The Obituaries in *The Times*,' I told her.

'Well, that makes a change!' Hilda gave me one of her small, disapproving clicks as she poured the tea.

'I always read the Obituaries in *The Times*,' I explained to her. 'They make me bloody glad to be alive.' I gave her a quotation from a particularly pleasing obituary. ' "Sir Frederick Foxgrove was known and respected as a wise judge and just sentencer. His behaviour in Court was always a model of dignity." In other words, old Foxy was Judge Jeffries without the laughs.'

'Is that really *lively* enough reading for you, Rumpole?' I saw She looking at me with a kind of sadness, and I answered, puzzled.

'The Obituaries can never be lively reading, exactly. Are you feeling quite all right, Hilda?'

'I'm not sure, Rumpole,' she sighed. 'Are you?'

'What?'

'Feeling quite all right.' She took a sad swig of tea and then went on to speak as though there were death in the family. 'Because if you're not, for any reason, I asked Dr MacClintock to drop in for a glass of sherry this evening. He'll be passing us on his rounds.'

'Damned expensive sherry, won't it be?' I could see no possible point in our pouring drink down the medical profession.

'Oh no, Rumpole. He's dropping in purely as a friend. I thought you could discuss with him any little worries you may have ... about anything ... at all.'

I didn't see how Dr MacClintock could possibly help me to get hold of the brief in R. *v*. Simpson, or indeed in any important matter. I rolled up *The Times* and prepared to go off to work. 'I'm catching an early train to Grimble tomorrow,' I warned Hilda. 'I may have to stay up there for a night or two.'

'Grimble? What on earth are you going to Grimble for?' My wife looked totally fogged. I suppose the answer I gave her was somewhat oblique.

'Sex! Some would say sex. Some would say the freedom of speech.'

And as I left to go about my business, I heard Hilda click her tongue again, sigh and say, 'Oh dear! I really think you'd better speak to Dr MacClintock about it.'

When I came, at last, to the end of a not very busy day (briefs were hardly showering in on Rumpole's return), I decided to give my favourite watering-hole, Pommeroy's Wine Bar, a miss, mainly for hard financial reasons, and I went straight back to Casa Rumpole. There I was sitting with a bottle of take-away claret (sadly I seemed to be down to the last couple of dozen) with my shoes and jacket off, reading with envy and disgust the *Evening Standard*'s account of a particularly asinine cross-examination, part of a nice libel action in which Guthrie Featherstone was undeservedly appearing, when She pushed open the door and ushered in the gloomy medico who had us on his panel.

'Here's Dr MacClintock,' she said. 'Come for his sherry.'

Come for *my* sherry might have put it more accurately; but I thought I might as well cheer the old darling up with a glass of the nauseous and liverish brew Hilda's friend Dodo had sent us for Christmas, and which I never drink anyway.

'Sit down, Doctor,' I said. 'We run a little charitable bar here, for depressed quacks.' And added, when I saw the look on Hilda's face, 'Take no notice of me. I was only joking.'

'Well, I'd better leave you two men to get on with it,' said Hilda, about to depart. 'Rumpole, you'd do very well to listen to every word that Dr MacClintock has to say.'

So, as rare things will, she vanished. I looked at the Doctor, who seemed to be going through some kind of terminal embarrassment. I poured him a sherry, for which he seemed unreasonably grateful.

'Excellent sherry, Rumpole. Amontillado?'

'Pommeroy's pale plonk.' It seemed a shame to disillusion him. 'Look, Dr MacClintock. What *are* you doing, dropping in like this? Other than mopping up the Spanish-style gut-rot?'

'Rumpole, your wife Hilda came to see me ...'

'Feeling seedy, was she? I told her she should never have come back to England. Climate in Florida suited her *far* better.'

The Doctor gulped more sherry, which gave him the strength to murmur, 'She was concerned about *you*, Rumpole.'

'You really like that stuff?' I looked at the iron-stomached Doctor. Then I further cheered him by giving us each a refill of our respective stimulants.

'As I explained to Hilda,' the Doctor spoke in a kind of sepulchral whisper. 'It's nothing for you to be ashamed of.'

'I can't say that I've ever felt *ashamed* of drinking a glass of claret.' The man didn't seem to be making a great deal of sense to me.

'Everyone has their little kinks,' the Doctor suddenly informed me. 'Their little peculiarities. Sometimes a doctor wonders if there's any such thing as a *normal* man.'

'Do you, Doctor?' I sat and lit a small cigar. The medic was failing to hold my attention.

'I have been married to Marcia, as you know, for going on twenty years.' Was this the time for a confession? I didn't want to probe the good Doctor's private grief.

I confined myself to asking politely, 'How is your good lady?'

'And I can't say that I've never been tempted' – the Doctor was now gaining his flow – 'sorely tempted, even to throw it up, well, I won't say for a gymslip and a pair of pigtails ...'

I looked sadly at the wretched MacClintock. 'You, Doctor?' I didn't, of course, withold my pity. 'Even *you*? Sometimes I think the whole world's going mad!'

'Hilda told me what you're doing. Try and see it in proportion, Rumpole. It's nothing to be guilty about.' He was now smiling at me in a sickly and reassuring way. I began to wonder if the man had been overworking.

'I don't feel particularly *guilty* about going to the north of England.' I did my best to reassure him.

'Of course not! That's probably a good idea. Bit of a winter break. Marcia and I went to Malta last year.' He then frowned as though an appalling thought had occurred to him. 'I say, Rumpole. You're not going to the north *with* anyone, are you?'

'No, of course not. What do you mean?'

'I shall be able to reassure Hilda. I told her I didn't think there was anyone who'd be interested in going to the north of England with *you*, Rumpole.'

'Is that what you came here to say?' My mind was starting to boggle.

'Yes. Yes, it is. I hope it's made you feel better.'

'As a matter of fact,' I had to be honest with him, 'it's made me feel considerably worse.'

'You're not to *worry*, Rumpole. We all have our own little guilty secret ...'

Then the Doctor, with the air of a man who has completed a painful duty, leant back and began to discuss the plans he had for insulating his loft. I imagine a lifetime of peering down various human orifices does, in the end, soften the brain; but I couldn't really understand why our neighbourhood G.P. had to work out his problems on our sherry.

Chapter Eleven

The next day I travelled up north to put up at the Majestic Hotel, Grimble (how well I remember that icy, marmoreal dining-room, the deaf waiters and the mattresses apparently stuffed with firewood), and to my struggle against censorship in the Grimble Crown Court. And Kenneth Cracknell, Esq., weary after a hard day at the Old Bailey, roared down to Brixton Prison on the Honda and there met his old friend and instructing solicitor Mike Mowbray and his client Percival Simpson, who looked at them, as Mowbray told me later, as if their visit had been a perfectly useless kindness and a complete waste of time.

'I can't fight against them.' Simpson sat at the table in the interview room and looked at them hopelessly. 'Not the miracle workers.'

'Now, Mr Simpson.' Young Mike Mowbray was trying his best. 'You've certainly got a difficult case. But Mr Cracknell's a barrister who's had a lot of success lately.'

'They can change the blood on a piece of paper. How can I fight against that?' Simpson smiled at them gently and then looked out of the window as if the case no longer held his full attention.

'Mr Cracknell has a whole lot of successful defences to his credit,' Mike went on gently.

'I have sinned. I appreciate that. What can I do?' Simpson gave another of his watery smiles.

'Mr Simpson. Who had the knife?' Cracknell felt he had to take some sort of command of this drifting conference, and came out with a pugnacious question.

'He gave me the knife. So I could kill myself. That's the cunning of *them*, you see,' Simpson said patiently, but apparently without any real hope of being understood.

'You had the knife, Mr Simpson. Now why did you use it? *Why*?' Ken was cross-examining his client, ever an unwise thing to do (you run the extreme risk of the old darling telling you he did the crime, which is hardly welcome information or helpful to the defence). At this point Mowbray was sure that he saw their client casually smother a yawn.

'I'm so *tired*,' Simpson admitted.

'Was it sex, Mr Simpson? Had he come down there to make sexual advances? Were you trying to fight him off?' Cracknell had, in his extreme lack of experience, hit on a somewhat trite defence.

'I must say, that was the line that appealed to me,' Mike Mowbray admitted, showing his prejudices. 'He was that sort of bloke, wasn't he? Eton and the Guards. That sort of character. Your Class A gay.'

'I don't know what sort of person he was, but he was one of *them*,' Simpson agreed.

'Well, exactly!' Mike Mowbray was delighted.

'I can't say any more really.' Simpson stood up to end the meeting. 'I'm tired of fighting ... Excuse me now, please. I can't say any more ...'

So it was a despondent Cracknell and Mowbray, counsel and instructing solicitor, who made their way out past the Alsatians and the trusty prisoners weeding the dusty plants in the black flowerbeds under the prison walls. As they approached freedom and the gate, Mike comforted his friend.

'You'll pull off something, Ken,' he said. 'You've always done that up till now.'

'On my own?' Ken sounded unexpectedly incredulous.

Mike was puzzled. He knew his friend was an ambitious young barrister, who wouldn't want to share the limelight which would shine on him in an important murder. 'You don't want a silk, do you?' he asked.

'Not a silk, no.' Ken Cracknell was thoughtful. 'But perhaps ... a very experienced member of the Junior Bar to lead me. You know, Mike. If you've got to insult an aristocratic corpse, grey hair might be a help.'

'An experienced junior?' Mike thought the suggestion over. 'Like who? You got any ideas?'

'Well, yes,' Ken Cracknell said, and I was amazed when I heard of it. 'I think I have.'

'Alderman Pertwee, did you visit the Adult Book Mart, Sowerby Street, on March 12th last?'

I was at home again, crowned by my old grey horsehair wig (bought second-hand from an ex-Attorney-General of Fiji in the 1930s) with the gown slipping off my shoulders and a collar like a blunt execution. In my sights, just alighted in the witness box, was a plump bird called Alderman Pertwee. He had a large stomach decorated with a gold watch and chain, ginger hair and moustache; he was small of stature and he had a beady and inquisitive eye. Our defence didn't in the least depend on the jury disliking Alderman Pertwee, but I thought that if Rumpole were ever to let him have it with both barrels, they might well be prepared to turn against him. Prosecuting counsel, a tall, skinny, young man named Mackwood, who was clearly horrified by *Schoolgirl Capers*, was leading the Alderman through his evidence-in-chief.

'I did visit the Adult Book Mart, your Honour.' The Alderman gave a small, corpulent and horribly ingratiating bow to the Judge before he answered the question. To his eternal credit the Judge rewarded him with a glassy stare of non-recognition. Pertwee then continued with his so-called evidence. 'I did, your Honour. And I found books and magazines of the most flagrant immorality on display.'

Now was the time to haul myself to my hind legs as in the days of yore. I spoke my first words in Court since my return. 'Your Honour, I object.'

'Yes, Mr Rumpole.' His Honour Judge Matthew was an amazingly civilized character for Grimble, although Albert had warned me that he was a tough sentencer. We had shared coffee and crossword clues the last time I had been up north and when he was still at the Bar, and he gave me a small, but quite charming, smile of welcome.

'If the Alderman could restrain himself from treating us like a Sunday night gathering at the Baptist Chapel,' I suggested, and his Honour took up the suggestion.

'Just confine yourself to the evidence,' he said courteously to the witness. 'It will be for the jury to decide on the exact nature of the articles for sale in the bookshop. Yes, Mr Mackwood.'

Mackwood asked his final question. 'Did you purchase at that shop the following articles: *Schoolgirl Capers* Volume I, numbers I to 6, *Double Dating in the Tower of Terror, Manacle Me, Darling* and the films the jury have already seen?'

'I did, my Lord.'

Mackwood subsided and Rumpole rose to cross-examine, looking hard at the jury and taking his customary ten seconds' pause before firing off the first question. 'Just a few questions, Alderman Launcelot Pertwee. You say this shop, the Adult Book Mart, is a source of corruption to the neighbourhood?'

'I regard it, your Honour' – another small bow, again ignored by the Judge – 'as a terrible source of corruption.'

'Standing as it does,' I put it to him, 'between a betting shop and the off-licence of the Grimble Arms, who's more corruptible, Alderman: the punters or the boozers?'

'I object! How can this witness possibly tell ... ?' Mackwood rose to his full height to make some alleged objection. I ignored him and he gradually subsided.

'Can't you, Alderman?' I kept my eye on the target witness. 'I thought you came here as an expert on corruption. Does not the Grimble Arms offer "Topless A-Go-Go" on the bar as an attraction on Friday nights?'

'I believe it does. Regrettable ...' Pertwee sighed in a pained sort of manner. I was delighted to see some of the jury smiling. Laughter is your strongest weapon against prosecutions of pornography. I made a reasonable suggestion to the Alderman.

'You don't think it might be preferable to have sex neatly packaged in books and magazines and not prancing about on the bar, kicking over the pints of Newcastle Brown?' There was laughter in Court, music to Rumpole's ears. 'Tell me, Alderman. There are no kindergartens, no convent schools, no academies for young girls of tender years in Sowerby Street, are there?'

'No, there are not, but ...'

'But me no buts, Alderman! And does not the Adult Book

Mart have written above the door in large letters, "Entry to those under 18 prohibited"?'

'I can think of no sign, Mr Rumpole,' said the Judge with a charming smile, 'that would be more immediately attractive to modern youth.' The jury rewarded him with a little titter. It was undoubtedly his Honour's point. I ignored him also.

'At least there were no kiddiwinks present when you went into the shop, were there, Alderman? No simpering maidens of bashful sixteen? No impressionable young students of theology? Not even the toughest teenager?'

'Not when I was there. No,' the witness admitted reluctantly.

'In fact the clientele consisted of three middle-aged men with suits, umbrellas and brief cases.' I put it to him, 'Perhaps they were all Aldermen of the fair city of Grimble?'

'They were all middle-aged men,' Pertwee admitted.

'Of perfectly respectable appearance?'

'I suppose so.'

'No one was actually slavering at the mouth, or walking with their knuckles brushing the linoleum?' I got home with a reasonable laugh then; the usher called, 'Silence!' and Mackwood looked extremely displeased and got to his hind legs.

'I really don't understand what my learned friend is getting at.' He made a self-consciously languid objection.

'Oh, don't you?' I was anxious to help him out. 'My learned friend says that this rubbish ...'

'It's not rubbish, Mr Rumpole!' My client Meacher whispered deafeningly from the dock. 'It's adult reading matter of an erotic nature.'

I increased my volume to suppress the sound of my aggrieved client, and turned to the witness box. 'This unmitigated rubbish, Alderman Pertwee, which you encouraged by spending two hundred pounds on assorted magazines and films ... was it your ratepayers' money?'

'I took a float, yes.' The Alderman sounded defensive. 'When I made this investigation on behalf of my Committee.'

'Do the ratepayers of Grimble know, Alderman, that you're spending their hard-earned pennies on *Schoolgirl Capers*?'

There was another small stir of laughter, which the Judge interrupted. 'Mr Rumpole. If you defer the rest of your cross-examination until tomorrow, we might break off there and the jury will no doubt wish to examine the ... um ... literature.'

'If they must, my Lord.' It's no help for the defence in an obscenity case to have anyone actually *read* the works in question. 'I should make it clear that I don't rely on the exact nature of this rubbish. I rely on our historic freedoms. Above all on the freedom of speech.'

'I would like the jury to read every word of these books and magazines,' said the lanky Mackwood, determined to rub their noses in it.

'Very well,' I shrugged at the jury. 'The prosecution is always far more interested in sex than we are.'

So we parted, and I spent the evening drinking claret in the Majestic (it tasted faintly of red ink and was apparently iced) with my old clerk Albert Handyside. When I got to Court the next morning, I was told that the jury were still out 'reading'. (I must say that when they finally returned to Court, some of the young men and women of the twelve seemed to have struck up friendships of a warmth over and above the call of jury service.) I also noticed that Albert and the client Meacher were in close conversation outside the Court with a tall, bony-looking red-haired woman who was wearing a luxurious mink stole and several large diamond rings, court shoes and a small hat with a veil. As he was talking, Albert seemed to be taking notes. Not wishing to interrupt him, and having no doubt that he was at work on another case, I went to a call-box and telephoned the mansion flat and She Who Must Be Obeyed.

'Rumpole, when are you coming home?' The tones were not over-friendly.

'Maybe a day or two. Not that we're *doing* very much. Everyone's sitting around, taking it easy and reading pornography.'

'Reading pornography?' Hilda sounded incredulous.

'Yes, of course. What else would you like us to do?'

'Oh, do be your age, Rumpole!' Whereupon Hilda slammed down the receiver.

Somewhat disconcerted by this I wandered back into Court. The jury was not yet back and Alderman Pertwee was sitting alone in a seat near the witness box, waiting to continue his evidence. He looked an unhealthy colour (bluish, I thought, around the edges) and was continually wiping his hands on a large white handkerchief. He also looked at the Court door from time to time in a nervous manner, and when he saw me his jaw dropped and his eyes became glassy. Not wishing to distress the wretched Alderman more than was absolutely necessary, I left the courtroom again and saw the red-headed woman apparently finishing her conference with Albert.

'Very well, Mr Handyside,' she was saying in a Grimble accent. 'I want you to handle the divorce. I want the whole town to know the truth about my husband. And I want them to know it as soon as possible. Do I make myself clear?'

'Absolutely clear, thank you *very* much,' said Albert and added, much to my surprise, 'And a very good day to you, Mrs Pertwee.'

'What?' I asked, coming up to Albert and the beatifically smiling Meacher. 'What did you call her?'

'He called her Mrs Pertwee,' said Meacher in a voice of unmistakable triumph. 'And he called her that because that's who she bloody is.'

'She came about a divorce. But she wants you to use her statement to cross-examine her husband this morning. As soon as Court sits.' Albert's eyes were now shining with a rare excitement. 'She can't wait to read all about it, it's bound to make front page of the *Grimble Echo*.'

'We've got him.' Meacher was grinning broadly. 'Mr Rumpole, we've got Alderman Purity Pertwee by the short and curlies!'

Albert leafed through his notebook, in which, it seemed, he had been taking a statement from the local Savonarola's wife. 'It does seem to be very valuable material, Mr Rumpole. Mrs Pertwee phoned me and I arranged to meet her here, early this morning. I'm gratified to say, sir, she gave me all the dirt.'

'She was miffed he wasn't taking her to his Ladies' Night at the Lodge. He told her she'd let him down. Launcelot

Pertwee told his old woman she always gets pissed on sherry at Masonic do's, that her face goes red and she's not fit to appear as an Alderman's wife. Silly sod. He's played straight into our hands.' Meacher was elated.

'So she gave me the whole story.' Albert proffered his notebook.

'Read it, Mr Rumpole! It'll make your hair stand on end. Shocked me, it did,' Mr Meacher admitted. 'I'm used to a respectable business.'

'He's keeping this young girl at Pond End. That's been going on for years, to her certain knowledge.' Albert was obviously only giving me a taste of the dish he had prepared, a little slice off the end of the joint.

'And Mrs Pertwee had to leave his bed because she failed to agree to certain practices. Have a look, Mr Rumpole.' Mr Meacher sounded pained but enthusiastic. 'And he attended a dubious film show after the annual do of the Management Committee of Grimble United.'

'Mrs Pertwee's found her clothes missing on several occasions. He's actually donned articles of her clothing.'

'He can't be left. Not even with the young girls who man the pumps at the garage he owns. They call him "Forecourt Freddie" because he's always out there chatting them up.'

'Lucky his Honour knocked off when he did. You can use all this stuff on the Alderman when we go back.'

Albert was giving his legal opinion, when I startled them both by saying, 'No!'

'What?' Albert frowned, as though he were hard of hearing.

'No. We can't use it.' I now hoped I had made myself clear.

'What do you mean, Mr Rumpole?' Meacher was determinedly reasonable. 'It's all good stuff, what Albert Handyside got you there.'

'Mr Meacher. I explained.' I did so again, quite patiently. 'We're going to win this case on liberty. The freedom of everyone to please themselves. To do as they like – provided they don't do it in the streets and frighten the horses. We are against peeping and prying through bedroom keyholes to censor and condemn our fellow human beings! If we attacked the Alderman for the shortcomings of his private life, we should be selling the pass. Don't you understand that? *We* should be the censors and the hypocrites. We should be selling our liberty!'

Meacher looked stunned, but Albert had the solicitor's immediate reaction: take counsel's advice and then you always have someone to blame if things go wrong. 'Of course, Mr Rumpole,' he said doubtfully. 'You're in charge.'

'Yes, I *am* in charge, aren't I? Don't be a back-seat driver, my dear old Albert, or you, Mr Meacher. Just sit back, relax and try to enjoy the view.'

So when we got back to Court, I told the Judge that I didn't wish to ask Mr Pertwee any further questions. The Alderman looked as though a reprieve had come through, and the sentence of death for which he had been preparing had been altered to a term of office as Mayor of Grimble. He bowed very low to the Judge, he actually contrived to bow to Rumpole, and went triumphantly out of Court.

As I had no intention whatever of putting my client Meacher in the witness box, the evidence was now over. After my learned friend Mr Mackwood had paraded his prejudices in a few ill-chosen words, I rose to make, although I say it myself, one of my very best speeches. I had, of course, had little else to think about and I had rounded the phrases during a long night listening to the central heating (far more noise than heat) in the Majestic Hotel. I won't weary you with the whole oration (the curious may find most of it only slightly misquoted in the *Grimble Echo* of the relevant date), but I will give you the end, the climax, the peroration. I included in it, of course, what is almost my favourite among Wordsworth's poems, dedicated to National Independence and Liberty.

> 'It is not to be thought of that the flood
> Of British Freedom, which, to the open sea
> Of the world's praise, from dark antiquity
> Hath flowed with pomp of waters unwithstood ...
> Should perish!'

I told the Grimble Jury.

I leaned forward then, dropped my voice and addressed them confidentially. 'Members of the jury. Freedom is not divisible. You cannot pick and choose with freedom, and if we allow liberty for the opinions we hold dear and cherish, we must allow the same privilege to the opinions we detest or even to works of such unadulterated rubbish as *Schoolgirl Capers* Volume 1, numbers 1 to 6. Let those who wish to read it do so; they will soon grow weary of the charms of such elderly schoolgirls. You and I, members of the jury, stand, do we not, for tolerance? We are not intolerant of Alderman Pertwee. He is free to express his opinions. We don't seek to call him a hypocrite, or have him banned.'

Young men and girls in the jury were sitting close together, some may even have been holding hands. I smiled at them. I think they may have smiled back. So I ended my speech.

'Ours is the tolerant approach, and if we are tolerant in great matters, so we must be in the little, trivial matter of these puerile magazines, for once we start in the business of censorship and the banning of books, that is the ending of freedom. Our priceless liberties are in your hands today, members of the jury. There could be no safer place for them!'

In due course the Judge summed up, with devastating fairness, and in due course the jury, having exchanged telephone numbers and arrangements for the weekend, struck their mini blow for respectability and found Mr Meacher guilty on all counts. The Judge dropped about nine pounds of charm and sent him to prison for 'polluting the fair city of Grimble'. It was a disappointed Rumpole, feeling every year of his age, who made the unpleasant trip to the cells which every barrister is in honour bound to take after his client has been convicted. And Meacher, I felt sure, wasn't going to prove a good loser; not for him the stiff upper lip of the playing fields of Eton. He was bloody angry, and he had no doubt where the blame was to be laid. As I entered the small cell under Grimble Court with a depressed-looking Albert Handyside, Mr Meacher muttered bitterly, 'Eighteen months!'

'Try and look on the cheerful side, Mr Meacher. You'll be in an open prison, hobnobbing with bent coppers, twisted solicitors and all the toffs.' I saw that I wasn't cheering him up.

'I wouldn't be in no sort of prison if you'd done your job properly.'

'You didn't like the speech?' I was, I must confess, a little disappointed by the client's reaction.

'I told you how to treat that bastard Pertwee. Go for the jugular!'

'It was Mr Rumpole's decision ...' Albert was going to do his best, but his disappointment was also clear. And he was interrupted by an explosion from Meacher.

'How can pissing Pertwee be on the Council? Lay bloody preacher. Chairman of the Watch Committee. And that Judge gave me eighteen months for polluting the fair city of Grimble.'

'Now that, I grant you, was a bit steep,' I sympathized with him. 'I don't know what he thinks this grimy and draughty northern borough is. I mean, the Station Hotel may have a sort of macabre Gothic charm, but otherwise ... Well, Grimble's hardly Venice in the springtime.'

'Anyway, I'm going to appeal!' Meacher clenched his fists and looked enormously determined.

'Now that, in my opinion, would be perfectly hopeless,' I told Meacher, and I had no doubt on the subject.

'I don't give a damn for your opinion, Mr Rumpole. You get me a young brief, Mr Handyside. Someone with a bit of guts, who'll tell the truth about Launcelot bloody Pertwee!' From his bench in the cell Meacher looked up at me, I thought malevolently. 'You're just like the old punters we get in our shops, Mr Rumpole, you are. Blokes what is past it.'

So it was in no light-hearted mood that I returned, travel stained, British Railway bashed, and jury battered, to my refuge in Froxbury Mansions. I had expected, on recent form, a cold welcome from She Who Must Be Obeyed. Imagine my surprise therefore, when I let myself in to the flat and found, in my living-room, lights dim, flowers bought and set in a cut-glass vase, and She reclining by the gas fire wearing some sort of dressing-gown. Our old wireless set was on, and from it the disembodied voice of the late Richard Tauber percolated, singing:

'Come, come, I love you only
My heart is true ...
Come, come, my heart is lonely
I long for you ...'

or words to the like effect.

As I entered the unexpectedly warm gloaming of our living-room She said, 'Rumpole, is that you, dear?'

'*What* did you call me?' I couldn't believe my ears.

'I called you "dear". Can't I call you "dear", Rumpole?' She rose gracefully and actually poured me a glassful of Pommeroy's plonk; and it was a liberal measure.

'I suppose there's no reason why not.' I took a gulp and a sniff round. 'Is there a rather odd sort of smell in here?'

'Is there ... ?'

'Distinctly unusual smell. Mixture of R.C. churches and old flower vases.'

'Well, that's not very romantic.'

'No.'

'I'm wearing lavender water, Rumpole,' Hilda said, almost coyly. 'The lavender water you give me every Christmas.'

'Sorry, I didn't recognize it.' I realized I had said the wrong thing, and returned my nose to my glass.

'Since we met, you have given me thirty-nine bottles of lavender water,' Hilda said without rancour.

'Well, I never knew what else you'd like to smell of.' And then I confessed, 'The case at Grimble was an unmitigated disaster. Very unsatisfied client.' I sat on the sofa and grate-fully changed the subject. 'I say, have you got a cold or some-thing? Been in bed, have you, Hilda?'

'What *do* you mean?'

'You're wearing your dressing-gown.' I thought it was about time someone pointed it out.

'It's really more of a négligée ...' And to my amazement Hilda came and sat down quite uncomfortably close to me. In fact she was squashing up against my knee as I scratched the old sore of my disastrous day in Court.

'I made the mistake of appealing to the old English sense of freedom. Freedom's gone out of fashion in Grimble. That singer appears to be in some pain.' Herr Tauber's voice had risen to a painful squeal. I put him out of his misery and switched him off.

'That was "These We Have Loved".' To my alarm Hilda was squashing up against me even more. 'We're not too old, are we, Rumpole,' she almost whispered, 'to enjoy anything sentimental?'

'No.' I made a cautious admission. 'But ...'

And then Hilda said a surprising thing. 'You don't *have* to read those magazines, Rumpole,' she said. 'After all, you are *married*.'

'What magazines?' I wasn't entirely with her.

'A dreadful thing about schoolgirls. I found it behind the sofa cushions.'

I began to get a strange glimmering, a sort of clue to Hilda's incalculable behaviour over the last weeks. 'Good heavens!' I told her. 'I had to read that, yes. It was part of the evidence in my case.'

'Your *what*?' Hilda seemed taken aback.

'The obscenity case. The one I did at Grimble. Good God, Hilda. You don't think I enjoyed reading that rubbish, do you? I've never been so bored in my whole life.'

'Bored?' She sounded curiously disappointed. 'Is *that* what you were?'

'Well, naturally. *You* didn't read it, did you?' My mind began to boggle at the thought of Hilda reading solemnly through 'Changing Room Orgies'.

However, she shook her head vigorously, got up quickly and moved away from me. 'No, of course not,' she said. 'It was your work, was it? That's all it was ...'

'Absolutely all!' I assured her.

She moved to the door and snapped on the centre light. Then she became brisk and businesslike as she emptied an ashtray and turned down the fire. I was back with the old familiar She Who Must Be Obeyed and it was almost a relief. At least I knew where I was, and she was no longer squashing my knee.

'Well, I've got to get on,' said Hilda. 'No use hanging about in the living-room all night, chattering to you. I've got chops to get under the grill! And you can start laying the table, Rumpole. You really might lend a hand occasionally.'

When she had left the room, I saw that the tide had gone down in the bottle of Pommeroy's claret. I reached up to find a reserve bottle propping up the Criminal Appeal Reports on the top of the shelf. 'That sounds more like your old self, Hilda.'

'What did you say?' Hilda called from the kitchen.

'Just getting another bottle off the shelf, Hilda,' I said, and on that occasion I got away with it.

Chapter Twelve

After the resounding defeat I had suffered in the case of the
Grimble Adult Reading Mart, I didn't see young Cracknell
for some time; indeed I didn't seek out his company as I
thought he was bound to crow a little over my discomfiture,
and perhaps suggest that I might vacate 'the room' if all I could
do there was to plan the loss of cases. However, I continued
to haunt the clerk's room and the library, I called in to Pommeroy's for an evening refresher and I generally planned my
days so that I had a credible reason for leaving home at Froxbury Mansions early in the mornings and not returning until
nightfall.

One day as I wandered into the clerk's room in a somewhat
disconsolate manner and noticed that the mantelpiece was, as
usual, bare of briefs marked 'Rumpole', Henry gave me a bit
of extremely welcome news.

'Mr Bernard rang of Cripplestone, Bernard & Co. You're
wanted for a case at Brixton. Case of Timson.'

Timson! The word was music to my ears. The Timson
family were a notable clan of south London villains who had
each and every one of them provided work for me over the
years. They were a close-knit family who went into crime
as other families go into the law. The Timsons thought of
spells in the nick as a professional risk, they believed that a
woman's place was in the home and they were against the
permissive society. There is no greater loyalty than that of one
Timson to another, and they had all, when in varied degrees
of trouble, relied heavily on the services of Rumpole. It
was a tribute to the excellent system of jungle telegraph
which existed in the world of crime that Rumpole's return should already have become known to the regular clientele.

'*Bonjour*, Mr Rumpole. *Heureux de vous voir.* Keeping well in yourself, are you?'

Bertie was one of the older members of the Timson family. He was facing a charge of conspiracy to rob the Balham branch of the Steadfast Savings Bank, or, in the alternative, carrying house-breaking implements by night. During a recent spell in the Scrubs he had taken French lessons, and would insist on practising his linguistic skill on his legal advisers.

'It seems you were caught with the following articles in your car, Bertie,' I reminded him. 'One brace and bit, one monkey wrench, two hacksaws, three sticks of dynamite with fuses and four imitation firearms, to wit revolvers.'

'All that in my bleeding *voiture*, Mr Rumpole!' Bertie Timson looked incredulous. 'Never!'

'The jury aren't going to believe you didn't have this stuff in your car. Not if three officers say they saw it there.'

'I do assure you, Mr Rumpole ...'

'Now it may be that you have an innocent explanation for some of these objects. The carpenter's tools, for instance?'

'An innocent explanation? *Entendu*, Mr Rumpole. I'll think about it.'

'You do that. Oh, and Bertie. *Dépêchez-vous!*'

'Come again, Mr Rumpole?'

'Think as soon as you can. Before your case comes up at London Sessions.'

Meanwhile, back at Chambers, life was filled, as usual, with intrigue and indeed romance. Guthrie Featherstone, who, as I have already indicated, had found the charms of our Portia, Miss Phillida Trant, increasingly irresistible, called on her in her room quite early one morning to find her boning up on the law of evidence preparatory to another day with her fraudsman.

'You're not still in that dreary case down at the Old Bailey, are you?' Featherstone asked gallantly.

'Yes, thank God. With some quite decent refreshers.'

'Pity.' Featherstone moved stealthily nearer to Miss Trant's desk. 'We might have had lunch tomorrow. Taken a trip along to the Trattoria Gallactica in the Fulham Road. You know. That's where all the B.P.s go.'

'The what?' Miss Trant was deep in Phipson's *Law of Evidence*.

'Beautiful People. Like you, Miss Trant. Won't you let me take you to lunch there?'

'I don't think so.' Miss Trant turned a page. 'What would your wife Marigold have to say?'

'I'm not exactly under her eagle eye at lunchtime.' Featherstone sniffed appreciatively. 'What a *super* perfume you're wearing. Do you know "Ma Tendresse"?'

'No. Who's she?'

'Oh, I say. Enormously witty. "Ma Tendresse". It's an absolutely *super* new perfume. Definitely exotic. You should try it.'

'I might ask Claude. But he's not much of a one for buying perfume.'

'No. That's the problem with barristers who get keen on commercial law. They lose the talent for giving perfume.' Featherstone smiled and then allowed his hand to fall casually on Miss Trant's shoulder as he approached the other object of his visit, secondary to the wooing but still of importance. 'Oh, I say, Miss Trant. I think you should know. I thought we might take on a new young member of Chambers. Apparently a brilliant cross-examiner.'

'Oh, really?' Miss Trant was still into Phipson and appeared not to notice Guthrie's hand.

'Yes. I thought you might know her. Her name's Elizabeth Chandler.'

At which Miss Trant shut her book and stood, dislodging Guthrie's grasp and said, with marked disapproval, 'A woman?'

'Probably,' Featherstone conceded. 'If the name's Elizabeth Chandler.'

'Oh, I don't think we want *another* woman in Chambers.' Miss Trant was firm on the subject.

'You don't? How very interesting.'

'Henry has to explain to solicitors about it being a woman he's sending down to the indecent assault. He often gets objections.' Even Featherstone was surprised at the speed at which an ambitious woman can, in the legal profession, show signs of Male Chauvinist Piggery.

'But you, Miss Trant. You're doing so marvellously well!' He smiled at her ingratiatingly.

'Well, I do flatter myself I've been accepted. But I don't think we need another *woman*.'

Featherstone was not displeased with this objection, seeing in it the chance of another meeting. 'Why don't we have a long, long chat, Miss Trant, as to exactly what we *do* need. And I'd like to discuss your life in the law. Old Keith was telling me the Lord Chancellor's office has definitely got its eye on you.'

'On *me*? You must be joking.' Miss Trant looked at her Head of Chambers somewhat more kindly.

'Oh no, Miss Trant,' Featherstone assured her. 'I'm not joking at all. Shall we say next Tuesday? At the Trattoria Gallactica, among the Beautiful People?'

The truth of the matter was that not only did Miss Trant feel that her distinguished position as the only woman in the all-male enclave at Equity Court was threatened; but she was particularly reluctant to admit Miss Elizabeth Chandler, a very warm-hearted blonde who hunted, got sent boxes of chocolates by judges, and conducted her cases with a beguiling mixture of pure law and smouldering sexuality which was quite a match for Miss Trant's courtroom performance. Miss Trant had also, during the time it took him to graduate from squatter to tenant, conceived something of an uncontrollable passion for Ken Cracknell, and she wasn't going to have Miss Chandler luring her impressionable young radical off to Point-to-Points and Hunt Balls and other such sinks of iniquity at the weekends. She raised the matter with Cracknell as they walked together down Fleet Street towards the Old Bailey.

'I don't know what Guthrie Featherstone thinks he's up to. I mean, we're packed like sardines in Chambers as it is.'

'We certainly are.' Ken was sunk in moody and sullen thought. Then he said, 'You did tell me Rumpole left the Bar because he was losing all his cases?'

'In front of Bullingham, yes. It depressed him dreadfully, but I think it was just a run of bad luck. It was bound to end sometime.'

'But he lost his nerve?'

'Yes.'

'And might lose it again. I mean, if he comes any more croppers.'

'I know.' Miss Trant looked at him with sympathy. 'He lost your dirty books case in the north. I think that's shaken him too.'

'How much more do you think it'd shake him, if he lost a really big one?' Cracknell asked thoughtfully.

'Well, badly.' They crossed the traffic and walked up to the dome and the lady with the sword, past the Black Marias and taxis loaded with dubious company directors converging on the Old Bailey. 'But about this ridiculous idea of Featherstone's. I really think I'll have lunch and talk him out of it ...'

So Miss Trant rattled on about her fears and indignation, but Ken Cracknell was hardly listening to her, his mind being on something else entirely.

Not long afterwards I was summoned, together with Bernard, my instructing solicitor, back to Brixton Prison for a second audience with Bertie Timson, whose fertile mind had in the interval provided him with some sort of a defence.

'I've been thinking about that load of stuff in the *voiture*, Mr Rumpole,' Bertie started thoughtfully.

'I'm glad to hear it, Bertie.'

'I've been remembering ...'

'I had hoped you would.'

'Them things were all to do with members of the family. Know what I mean?' It didn't seem a particularly difficult conception and I grasped it. 'Them hacksaws and the brace and bit ...'

'Not tools for the bank robbery?' I asked.

'D.I.Y.'

I was at sea, in a world of initials. 'Come again?'

'Do It Yourself, Mr Rumpole. Den's Monica was getting married and moving into a mobile home near Harlow. I was going to do up their bathroom.' I wondered what sort of lorry it might have been, off the back of which a mobile home might have dropped as a wedding gift, but I was too polite to interrupt Bertie's flow. 'I was going to give her shelves with concealed lighting and a wooden surround for the bath. *Très élégant.*' Bertie seemed pleased with his explanation and rounded it off in French. 'The toy guns was presents for my sister Vi's kids.'

'I don't want to ask awkward questions ...'

'Mr Rumpole, I know you don't.'

'But the sticks of dynamite?'

'You want to know the truth?' That was a question I thought it wiser to leave unanswered, so I let Bertie continue. 'My cousin Cyril's got a cottage down in rural Essex. Charming little place. But the fact is ... I don't want to shock the ladies in the jury.'

'Carry on, Bertie,' I said. 'Have no fear.'

'No main drains, Mr Rumpole. Nothing but a septic affair down the end of the garden. And *malheureusement* this tank gets blocked up ... it won't seep away, not as it's meant to. And Cyril's old woman Betty, she gets on to him about this. But how do you unblock a septic tank, Mr Rumpole?'

'I can't really say I've given the matter any thought.'

'Dynamite. That's the idea I hit on.'

'Sounds a desperate solution ...'

'Cyril's Betty was getting desperate, Mr Rumpole. So I happened to meet this Welsh geezer, who works in the quarries ...'

'A bloke whose name you can't remember, but you happened to meet in a pub?' I suggested, a little wearily.

'How did you know that, Mr Rumpole?' Bertie looked pained.

I might have said, 'From a long experience of Timson family defences.' But I thought it more tactful to keep quiet.

'So this geezer said he had a bit of dynamite to spare, like, and I bought a few sticks off of him. I put them in the car for next time I was going down to Cyril and Betty's for a country weekend. I'd actually forgotten all about them, if you want to know the truth.'

There was a pause as I thought our defence over, then I said, 'Could we call Betty Timson as a witness?'

'Oh no, Mr Rumpole. She wouldn't want to come to Court.'

It was all rather as I had suspected. I sighed and lit a small cigar. 'So that's the story?'

'*Exactement*, Mr Rumpole.'

I blew out smoke and heaved myself to my feet. 'Well, we'll do what we can with it. I can't make any promises. It's a bit more convincing than a complete denial, I suppose.'

I got back from my second conference with Bertie Timson in Brixton Nick, pushed open the door of the common room and found it to be fully inhabited and stinking of some foul tobacco that Ken Cracknell rolled himself to show his solidarity with the working man (who was probably smoking low-tar filter-tip Health Hazards, anyway). Ken was sitting at the desk and Glendour-Owen filled the armchair with himself and a large brief.

I had, as I have said, rather avoided a confrontation with Ken Cracknell since the Grimble débâcle, but now that it could no longer be avoided I decided that the only way was to come clean, confess that I'd been got bang to rights and hope for a conditional discharge.

'Oh, Ken,' I greeted him. 'Do you mind if I call you Cracknell? I'm afraid I didn't do too well up in Grimble.'

'Henry told me.' Cracknell leant back in my swivel-chair and put his feet firmly on my desk.

'A dissatisfied client, I'm sorry to say.'

'Yes.' Cracknell glowered at me and then, quite unexpectedly, he smiled. 'Well. I don't expect it was your fault.'

'It seems Rumpole spouted Wordsworth at the jury. It went down like a lead balloon.' The small Celtic person giggled from my armchair.

'I found the result ... a little disappointing,' I confessed.

'There'll be other cases.' To my amazement I got the distinct feeling that Ken Cracknell was trying to cheer me up.

'Meacher's got twenty dirty book shops, all coming up for trial.' I didn't want to conceal the extent of the damage. 'I doubt if I'll get a brief in any of them.'

There was a long silence. Cracknell was still smiling, but more to himself, I thought, than to anyone in the outside world. He took out his cigarette machine and a packet of that tobacco which makes old men cough so terminally on dawn tube trains round the Angel Islington. When he had lit his next offensive cigarette, he said something which made me forgive his roll-ups, his boots on my table, his awful posters on my walls and even made me ready and willing to call him Ken. What he said not only justified my journey across the Atlantic but restored my faith in the law, in human nature, and even made me suspect that some benign Power might be keeping watch over old barristers. As he spoke, it seemed I heard bells ringing and even Owen Glendour-Owen was lapped in a roseate glow.

'I was thinking of asking you to lead me in my murder,' Cracknell said casually, blowing out a cloud of instant bronchitis.

'You ... ? Me ... ?' For once in my life I was incoherent.

Cracknell, from now on I shall call him Ken, went to my mantelpiece, took down the coveted brief in R. *v.* Simpson. 'I feel,' said the dear boy, 'that you're absolutely right for this.'

I didn't dispute it. It was a case which I always knew should have been mine.

'I mean, I don't want some smooth leader like Guthrie Featherstone who'll twist Simpson's arm and make him plead guilty.'

'Plead guilty?' I almost exploded. 'I never plead guilty!' At which I grasped the proffered brief before Ken had any chance of changing his mind.

'It's not an easy case, Rumpole.' Ken looked genuinely worried, bless his heart. 'I really don't know what the answer is.'

'Worry not, old darling. My dear Ken, your days of anxiety are over. The answer lies in the blood.'

Chapter Thirteen

I had a murder. I even had a suspected carrying of house-breaking implements by night. It's true that after our singular evening with Richard Tauber a certain amount of cold air had been blowing between myself and She Who Must Be Obeyed. I didn't feel I was forgiven for the sudden dash to freedom, nor was it likely to be forgotten in a hurry. As a consequence, there was a good deal of silence about the matrimonial home, broken, from time to time, only by the clicking of Hilda's tongue.

Once outside the confines of Froxbury Mansions, however, my spirits rose, my step was lighter and I could be heard to hum tunelessly as I emerged from the Temple tube station with the light of approaching battle in my eye. God was in his heaven and I had the brief in R. *v.* Simpson, and so there was nothing much wrong with the world outside Froxbury Mansions.

It was therefore with a feeling of exhilaration and excitement that I returned to that favourite rendezvous of mine, the interview rooms at Brixton Prison. Ken had made his own way by bike and young Mowbray had walked down from his nearby office. However, a few minutes with our client Percival Simpson served to lower my spirits. He sat very quiet in his grey clothes, staring through the glass partition at the screws' collection of cactus plants, and he seemed so utterly uninterested in the work at hand, so entirely resigned to his defeat and eventual conviction, that it was, I must confess, a little disappointing.

'It's a miracle,' he said at the outset, and seemed to find the thought depressing.

'Oh, I wouldn't say that, Mr Simpson. It may seem miraculous to you ...' I started modestly.

'What?' Simpson turned to me then, but without any particular interest.

'My being here!' That, I was sure, was the miracle he meant. 'A gift from heaven! Is that how it strikes you? Rumpole, who many believed was tucked away in some sunshine home, is back in the land of the living.' I lit a small cigar and continued. 'I have news for you, Simpson, old darling. You see, I received a letter about this little murder of yours, which has, I'm bound to admit, some fairly attractive features. And I came back in nothing more miraculous than the cut-price Gaelic Airlines Budget Special, which is a little like being shot across the Atlantic in a rather unclean corner of the tea bar at King's Cross...'

'About the blood.' Simpson didn't seem to be following me. 'That must be a miracle.'

'If you have one fault, Mr Simpson,' I told him reluctantly, 'it is that you are a touch too ready to assume the miraculous.'

'I can't fight it.' He shook his head in resignation.

'Oh yes, Mr Simpson, you can fight it and you will fight it.' It was going to be an uphill task putting a little spirit into this Simpson.

'You're going to ask me about what happened in the tube station...?' he sounded anxious.

'Am I?'

'I can't tell you about that. They'd never let me go if I told you that. They can work miracles, you see. They always told me they could.'

'They, Mr Simpson?' I was beginning to lose his drift. 'Who are "They"?'

'I can't say. I really ... can't say.' This time he shook his head and spoke with considerable decision.

'Never mind. All in good time. I'm sure you'll be able to.' I thought it best to gain his confidence by starting as far as possible from the unfortunate incident on the underground station. 'I was going to ask you a little about yourself. You work, don't you, in the office of the Inspector of Taxes, Bayswater Division?'

'Yes.' Simpson seemed this time, perhaps understandably, reluctant to admit it.

'That's not a criminal offence,' I reassured him. 'Although it'll hardly endear you to the jury.'

'I've always been good at figures. Since I was a child. Figures hold no mystery for me.'

'Keen on your work, are you?' As a constant victim of the Revenue's little brown envelopes, I found it hard to restrain a shudder.

'Oh, very keen.' Simpson began to look almost lively. 'Every Thursday evening after work I go to evening classes in Advanced Accountancy.'

I glanced at the brief, checked the day of the murder. 'You went regularly to your evening classes, by tube?'

'Well, I don't run to a car, Mr Rumpole.' Simpson continued to react almost like a living being.

'What about supper?'

'What?'

'What about your supper, when you went to evening classes?'

'I'd always buy a take-away chicken, and then I'd take the tube on to my bed-sit.'

'In Alexander Herzen Road?'

'Yes.'

'And that was your regular routine on Thursdays?'

'Yes, it was.'

It was important information, which I filed away in the back of my mind; but I was getting uncomfortably near the incident which I knew would sting Simpson to silence, so I asked a safer question. 'Who'll talk about your good character? Friends at work?'

'I don't know many people. They call me "The Duchess" in the Inland Revenue.'

'They *what*?'

'It's a bit of a joke on my name, I suppose. Mrs Simpson, you see. The Duchess. I suppose it's a bit of a funny joke ...'

'I see. Richly entertaining.' I smiled obligingly. 'You've always been in the tax-gathering business?'

'Since I left school at sixteen. I came in as tea boy in the Pay-As-You-Earn. Now I'm Number Two Accountant in the Schedule D.'

'A meteoric rise. And your spare time ... holidays? All that sort of thing?'

'Spare time? Well, it's television. And I bring work home.'

'Speaking as a taxpayer, Mr Simpson ... Duchess. Couldn't you manage to be a little less dedicated to your calling?' I said hopefully, and when he didn't answer I asked, 'What about holidays?'

'Holidays? I used to stay with my mother in Worthing, until she was gathered.' I managed to look suitably sympathetic, and then Simpson said, 'Only this year I managed a holiday abroad. I went to the Sunshine, on a package.'

'Sunshine?' I tried to keep the renewed hope and excitement out of my voice and said, as casually as possible, 'Not the Sunshine State, Duchess? That's not where they sent you on a package?'

'Yes, of course. Florida.' Simpson seemed to be losing interest again.

'Florida! Of course. You took your annual leave in Florida. Just when did it happen? Duchess ... just when and where did it happen?' Simpson didn't answer me, but he shook his head. 'All right. All right. You can tell me later,' I reassured him and then I stubbed out my small cigar and stood. I said the words I remembered. 'We shall meet and talk, friend and brother. As sure as the seed grows in the sunlight. We shall meet and talk.'

The effect was extraordinary. Simpson looked straight at me, his voice seemed forced and his eyes were full of fear. 'They sent you! They sent you ... to betray me!'

'Of course they didn't. Do get your mind off miracles, Mr Simpson. I told you ...' I was tying up my brief with its pink tape. 'I came on a "See the World" Budget Special of Gaelic Airlines. I came entirely of my own accord.'

Simpson didn't look reassured, but I thought there was nothing more I could say to convince him at that moment and that I had learnt all he was prepared to tell me.

Ken and Mowbray and I were sprung from Brixton. As we walked up the long, wet street that leads to the main road, past the little groups of mums and babies and girl-friends

98

come to visit their men in the nick, Ken asked if I thought our client was insane.

'Oh, really, Ken. Who's sane? You or I or the learned judge? Or the screws who've condemned themselves to life imprisonment?'

'All right, then. Is he fit to plead?'

'Of course he is. And he's fit to be acquitted.' I looked at Ken and thought that, in spite of my everlasting gratitude to him for bringing me in as his leader, the time had come for a little gentle criticism. 'I see by your brilliant cross-examination in the Magistrates Court that you were suggesting that Simpson did it while protecting his honour against a homosexual attack.'

'It seemed about the only line.' Ken was unusually modest.

'The Guardsman's Defence, eh? Seems a rather old-fashioned gambit for a bright young radical barrister.'

'You don't think it'll work, sir?' Michael Mowbray was respectful.

'I don't think a Guardsman's Defence works particularly well, if you happen to have a client whose nickname is The Duchess.'

We had reached the car park by the main road, and Ken's Honda was waiting for him. 'Want a lift ... ?'

'No, thank you. I had enough excitement on Gaelic Airlines.'

Ken armed himself in the huge helmet, strode the motor bicycle and thundered away. Young Mowbray gave me a sympathetic smile. 'Bit of a hopeless case, Mr Rumpole? Beginning to wish you were back across the Atlantic?'

'No, old darling. I don't wish that at all. Oh, you might start making a few tactful inquiries about the Hon. Rory Canter deceased.'

'About his sexual habits?' my young instructing solicitor asked eagerly, and looked quite disappointed when I said, 'Oh, dear boy, no. About his religion.'

There was only one thing to do now in the defence of Percival Simpson, and that was to telephone my son Nick on the other side of the Atlantic. So when I got back to Chambers, I sent instructions down to Henry to place the call, and he received them in a clerk's room crowded with Uncle Tom and Ken and Miss Phillida Trant. According to Miss Trant, this audience received the news from Henry that I was calling my son in America with a good deal of fascination and a certain amount of hope.

'Do you think Rumpole's contemplating doing the vanishing trick again?' Uncle Tom asked. 'Back into the sunset? I wonder if we'll have to give him another clock.'

He was referring, with some bitterness, to the occasion when Chambers had chipped in to buy me a clock against an earlier proposed retirement which never came off. 'Or is this another positively last appearance, like the ageing opera singer?' Uncle Tom went on, talking to no one in particular.

'It's working,' Ken said to Miss Trant, with a good deal of quiet satisfaction.

'What's working?' She wasn't sure if she followed him.

'Just an idea of mine,' said the young radical as he led her down to the Old Bailey and the endless fraud. 'Don't you worry your pretty head about it.'

'Dad. Yes, of course it's me. No ... I'm not at work. Because it's four o'clock in the morning. Well, no ... I haven't had your letter.'

I suppose I should have had more consideration for my daughter-in-law Erica, lying in the warm sleep of pregnancy, who was aroused at an ungodly hour to hear her husband Nick talking, in a bewildered sort of way, to the telephone.

'Street corner?' Nick was saying. 'What street? Handing out *leaflets*? And flowers? Yes. Yes, of course I'll try ... It's all ... all in your letter, is it? Well, anyway, you sound happy. Yes ... Yes ... Love to Mum.'

As Nick put down the phone Erica asked him, in some dread, 'He doesn't want to come back here, does he?'

'No,' said my son, and he sounded puzzled. 'No. He wants me to find Tiffany Jones.'

My Nick is a good lad, and indulgent to the whims of his no doubt trying father. Accordingly he was to be found, when the academic day finally began, in a corner of the tree-lined, bicycle-ridden campus, having a quiet talk with Paul Gilpin from the English Department.

'That last day you saw Tiffany, Paul. Did you notice anything unusual about her?'

'How do you mean, unusual?'

'She wasn't ill or anything?'

'No. She seemed well. Happier than ever. Only one thing. I noticed she'd cut her arm. She was wearing a band-aid. I did ask her about it and she wouldn't tell me.'

'You don't think it was a rusty needle?' Nick had had many unhappy examples of this among his students.

'Oh, come on, Nick. You know Tiffany wasn't like that.'

'And you haven't heard from her since then?'

'Not a single word.' Paul Gilpin was depressed, as anyone would be who is suddenly and mysteriously deprived of a life with a girl like Tiffany Jones.

'She never left a note, no message?'

'Not a thing.'

'It's worrying for you ...'

'I went mad to start with. Rang round the hospitals and the police, of course. But at least now I know she's alive.'

'How do you know?'

'Someone came round for her things.'

'They did?'

'Didn't I tell you? About three weeks ago, I guess. A guy called and said Tiffany wanted her things.'

'Who was he?'

'The guy who came?'

'Yes.'

'Pretty young. In his twenties, I guess. Nice-looking boy, but nothing you'd notice. Clean jeans and a clean white shirt. That sort of style.'

'He didn't tell you his name?'

'He didn't tell me a damned thing. Said he had strict instructions not to answer questions. Instructions from Tiffany, I guess. I found that very hurtful. Also I thought it was a little strange. The things that she wanted.'

'What did she want?'

'Well, certainly not clothes, make-up, none of the things you'd think a girl might need. He just took her books on math, slide-rule, pocket calculator. Just the things she uses for her work in statistics and economic forecasts.'

'The tools of her trade?'

'Exactly that.'

Chapter Fourteen

Whilst Nick was pursuing his researches into the strange disappearance of Tiffany Jones, and I was hanging round our clerk's room in the hope of picking up any crumbs in the shape of discarded dangerous drivings or superfluous solicitings, Miss Trant kept her luncheon appointment with our somewhat flustered and overexcited Head of Chambers Guthrie Featherstone in the Trattoria Gallactica in the Fulham Road. I owe the following account of this meeting to her subsequent description of it to me over a glass of Pommeroy's plonk.

Featherstone was wearing a new silk tie and had obviously been waiting some considerable time. He was nervously snapping breadsticks between his fingers when Miss Trant arrived the regulation fifteen minutes late. As she sat down, she noticed a brimming campari soda and a gift-wrapped package by her plate. Gulping the one and tearing at the sellotape with inquisitive fingernails at the other, she asked, 'Is this for me?'

'I bought it for you. Yes,' Featherstone admitted.

'What an enormous bottle!' Miss Trant had succeeded in unshrouding what seemed to be a pint or two of 'Ma Tendresse'.

'Well. It's only the toilet water, I'm afraid. I mean, who wants to spend twenty pounds on a bottle of the perfume? I mean, when you get so much more ... with the toilet water.' Featherstone was struggling, ill-advisedly, with the economics of the situation.

'Exactly. Well, I'll slosh it around,' Miss Trant said cheerfully. 'It'll probably absolutely slay them down at the London Sessions.'

'I bought it for you especially. "Ma Tendresse", from Harrods. Claude won't mind you wearing it?'

'Claude's not terribly into perfume,' Miss Trant admitted,

and then went into the subject which was uppermost in her mind. 'Now, about the girl you're thinking of taking into Chambers.'

'Marriage!' Featherstone's mind was on other things. 'It's a funny thing about marriage. Marigold and I, we have our different interests. Marigold's taken up choral singing. They're doing the *Saint Matthew Passion*.'

'Oh yes. And what passion are you doing, Featherstone?' Miss Trant looked at her host with some suspicion.

Featherstone, thinking he was being treated like a dangerous Don Juan, was flattered. 'I say, you *are* sharp, aren't you? But look here, Phyllis. Do call me Guthrie.'

'Phillida.'

'What?'

'My name's Phillida. You see, I've been making inquiries about this Elizabeth Chandler person, and I'm not at all sure she's the type that would really muck in at Chambers. Also, there are only a certain number of matrimonial disputes where solicitors *want* women. I mean, are there enough for two?'

'Matrimonial disputes,' Featherstone said gloomily. 'Well, there are quite enough of those, God knows. But Marigold and I, we just face facts.'

'What facts?' Miss Trant asked without interest.

'Well, we may fancy other people. And well, other people might fancy us.'

'Might they?' Miss Trant's neutral tones didn't betray her incredulity.

'We only stick together, of course, for the sake of the children.'

'Oh. I hadn't heard about the children.'

'Hadn't you really?' Featherstone suddenly became a great deal more relaxed. They had got on to a subject on which he felt thoroughly at home. 'Well, there's Arabella. She goes to this funny little school in Kensington. I mean, she's eight, but she's already got this extraordinary talent for dancing. And little Luke, well, he's only just three, but I've got him down for Marlborough. I imagine he might want to come to the Bar some day.'

'You don't want to fill the Chambers up with Elizabeth

Chandler, then?' Miss Trant was quite uncertain as to whether she had scored a victory.

'Look. If you've never actually seen the children, I just happen to have a couple of photographs about me. Only snaps, of course. We took them in Portofino last long vacation. It wasn't frightfully sunny weather. That's Bella on the terrace of our hotel.' Featherstone had produced his wallet, from which he proudly drew a number of creased and faded snaps from the space between his credit cards and his cheque book.

'What's she doing?' said Miss Trant, giving a cursory look. "The Dying Swan"?'

'Oh, yes,' said Featherstone proudly. 'Quite the little Margot Fonteyn, isn't she? And this is old Luke with his fingers in the spaghetti. Oh, my God!' Featherstone's voice had sunk to a hoarse whisper. He was staring across the restaurant at a couple of dark-suited businessmen who were about to settle at a distant table.

'What on earth's the matter?' asked Miss Trant, puzzled.

'My God! My God!' Featherstone moaned gently, his hand on his chest.

'Featherstone. Guthrie! Are you in some sort of pain?' Miss Trant was no Florence Nightingale, and hoped to God she wouldn't be called on to administer the kiss of life.

'Pain? Yes. Pain. That's what I'm in. Of course. I must dash. Immediately! Look, I'll pay the bill.' At which Featherstone stood up suddenly and pushed back his chair.

'Pay the bill? We haven't eaten anything!' Miss Trant pointed out reasonably, but Featherstone was on his way out of the Trattoria Gallactica, waving a limp hand and muttering vaguely, 'Goodbye, Phillida. See you in Chambers. Sometime.'

This highly unsatisfactory luncheon had an immediate effect which unexpectedly involved me, and in a most unwelcome manner. I had just lost a perfectly simple and winnable indecent assault in a cinema at Uxbridge, and was gloomily wondering if I had lost my grip. As I wandered into the clerk's room, Henry told me that there was a lady waiting for me upstairs. As I opened the door, I noticed a welcome absence of Ken and Glendour-Owen, and the unlikely presence of a

handsome woman, about thirty-five years of age with a cash-
mere twinset, a double row of pearls and an expression of
grim determination.

'Mr Rumpole. We have met, over the years. At Chambers
parties. I'm Marigold Featherstone.'

I remembered the wife of the Q.C., M.P., our Head of
Chambers. 'Of course. Look, I'll just see if Guthrie's in his
room.'

'I don't want Guthrie at this particular moment.' I thought
the tone was somewhat chilling. 'Thank you very much. It's
you I want, Mr Rumpole. Would you mind closing the door?'
Hers was a tone of command. I shut the door behind me.

'You want *me*, Mrs Featherstone?'

'Tell me, Mr Rumpole. Do you handle divorce?'

'Only rarely. And then with particularly thick gloves. Why
do you ask?' I sat down at my desk.

'I ask, Mr Rumpole, because I have need of your services.'

'Of mine?'

'For a divorce.'

'I mean, who ...' I thought she perhaps had a lady friend
tossed on the rough seas of a stormy marriage, but her answer
set me rocking back in the swivel-chair.

'My husband, Mr Rumpole. I'd hardly be bothering to
divorce anyone else's husband, would I?' I could see the force
of her argument. 'I'm afraid Guthrie's gone completely off the
rails.' She sighed, and had she been my Hilda, she would
have undoubtedly clicked her tongue. 'He has taken up, Mr
Rumpole, with another woman.'

'Oh, well now. Can you be sure about that? I mean, what's
the evidence?' I couldn't see a man, even Guthrie Featherstone, suffer such a summary conviction.

'The evidence, Mr Rumpole,' Mrs Featherstone said impas-
sively, 'is the evidence of my own eyes.'

From that moment I began to feel pessimistic about the
chances of any sort of defence for our learned Head of Chambers. The eyes of his lady wife were clear and unblinking,
the sort of eyes that might well be believed in a court of law.
She continued with her evidence.

'I was in the perfume department at Harrods, Mr Rumpole.

I was buying my usual little atomizer. Guthrie never brings *me* perfume home, and I happened to catch sight of him, at the "Ma Tendresse" counter.'

'He was buying perfume?' I hazarded a guess.

'Well, Mr Rumpole. He wasn't buying potatoes.'

I began to see that there was a certain ruthless logic about this woman's mind. I asked the obvious question. 'Did you confront him?'

'I moved towards him, but Harrods was extremely crowded on that day and he escaped. Furtively.'

'Did you ask him about it?'

'No.'

'Why?' Poor old Guthrie had no doubt been condemned without a hearing.

'I didn't want to give him the chance to lie to me.'

A woman of steel, you'd have to agree, this Mrs Marigold Featherstone. However, I did my best to sound unconvinced by the evidence. 'Well, I don't see that adds up to much of a case. He might have been buying scent for anyone, an old aunt perhaps. Has he got an old auntie with a birthday?'

'He was buying it, Mr Rumpole,' said Marigold, driving the final nail into her husband's coffin, 'for the girl he took out to lunch at the Trattoria Gallactica.'

'Oh yes?' I did my best to sound casual. 'And which girl was that?'

'Some little tart. I don't know her name. My brother Tom was lunching his accountant at the Trattoria Gallactica, and he distinctly saw Guthrie at the corner table gazing into the eyes of this King's Road strumpet. And do you know what Tom saw plonked on her plate?'

'Tagliatelle verdi?' I was guessing again, of course.

'A great big bottle of "Ma Tendresse". The toilet water. Of course, as soon as he caught sight of Tom, Guthrie simply got up and legged it. He's a terrible coward, you know.'

The wretched Featherstone clearly needed the assistance of a good lawyer. Always ready to take on a hopeless case, I decided to defend him. 'Mrs Featherstone. If I were to act for you in this dispute with your husband ...' I started cautiously.

'Yes?' said Marigold eagerly.

'The Head of Chambers! Well, it would cause enormous embarrassment.'

'If I'm divorcing Guthrie, Mr Rumpole, embarrassment is just what I intend to cause!' This was not a woman to be trifled with.

I said, 'Leave it with me, Mrs Featherstone. I'll think it over.' A bit of delay, I had found it an infallible rule, never does any harm to the defence.

'I shall call on you next week,' said Marigold Featherstone coldly. 'Then I shall expect your answer.'

Whilst I set about the unlikely task of finding a defence to the charges brought by this implacable plaintiff against our Head of Chambers, my son Nick, out of the extreme goodness of his heart, was finding out some other answers for me. He climbed into his rather battered Volkswagen (Erica kept the estate car for her use) and drove down to the Miami shopping street where I had been buying small cigars when I first heard about seeds growing in the sunlight.

Nick parked his car and walked up and down the street, but drew a blank. Then he went into a bar and ordered a cold beer and sat staring at the intersection I had recommended to him, but saw nothing unusual. He ordered another beer without incident; but when it came, and he was about to lower his mouth to the tooth-freezing and gaseous liquid, he saw two girls in white dresses come into the bar carrying long-stemmed chrysanthemums. Nick looked, as he told me, and saw the young man in the white shirt and tie standing at the street corner with the flowers which he handed out to the passers-by, all of whom received them and his greetings with politeness and some with interest.

In a moment Nick had abandoned his beer and was standing in front of the young man who had just presented him with a chrysanthemum.

'It's a sunshine day,' said the young man cheerfully.

'Is it? I really hadn't noticed,' Nick said with carefully affected gloom.

'Sunlight to Children of Sun,' said the young man. 'Are you not aware of the sun, our source of strength?'

'I guess I'm only aware of my problems. I've sure got a few of those.' Nick was giving an excellent performance of a young American academic going through a crisis in his personal relationships.

'Meet and talk.' The young man was smiling and interested.

'Pardon me?' said Nick, apparently lost in dejection.

'We shall meet and talk, friend and brother,' the young man repeated, 'as sure as the seed grows in the sunlight.'

'Meet and talk?' Nick looked up gratefully.

'Well, sure thing, friend and brother. You and I have all the time in the world for one-to-one communication. You haven't done much talking lately? Just exchanged words, is that it? Not real talking.' The young man looked at Nick in a kindly and yet penetrating way, and Nick agreed quickly.

'Exchanged words. Yes. That's exactly it!'

'That's all you do on the outside, isn't it?' The young man in the tie nodded understandingly. 'Exchange words in the office, or with your family maybe. But never talk, one heart to another's heart, beating as one. They never know that, the Children of Dark.'

'It's just that I've been feeling terribly lonely lately,' Nick admitted in evident distress.

'Come with me then, friend and brother. The lonely days are over. Come with me, and we'll talk it all through.'

Nick's troubles were apparently serious enough for the young man to shut up the free chrysanthemum service and suggest a walk on Miami beach. He took a lift in that direction in Nick's German antique, and then they walked, two young men in close and confidential conversation, past the bejewelled geriatrics and the golden lads and girls who were presently leaping about at volley ball, or stretched beautifully on towels. In what seems, when you have passed through it, to be a regrettably short period, these golden lads and girls would be in need of hearing aids, bifocals and a cheap blood pressure service.

'What's your name?'

'Nicholas Rumpole.'

'Then you're Nicholas.'

'What's yours?'

'You can just call me William. That's my given name. My family name's forgotten now. A family name's the first thing we give up, we Children of Sun. But then we forget a lot of things.'

'Children of Sun?' Nick sounded puzzled.

'We shall inherit the earth. We Sun Children.' William looked at Nick and he was smiling.

'Sounds interesting. When?'

'In ten years. William had no doubt about it. 'When the time of Darkness is over, the world shall belong to the Sun's Children.'

'It's a religion?' Nick hazarded a guess.

'It's a whole life.'

'Christian?'

William shook his head. 'Jesus is no use to us. Jesus died. We're not interested in death, Nicholas. Death or sickness. We shall give back health to the world, during the years of Rule.'

'The years of *what*?'

'First we have the years of Preparation,' William explained. 'Then the years of Rule, when the Sun's Children enter into their inheritance. You see, the Master gives us everything. He protects us with his power. His power for the miraculous.'

'Miracles?' Nick inquired simply.

'Oh, sure. *He*'s not bound by the laws of man and nature. *He* gives us perfect freedom, Nick. And in return what do we give him? Well, I guess we just about give him everything. Perfect loyalty. Perfect fidelity. And you know the joy, Nick? He gives us perfect peace.'

A little later they were sitting at a straw-roofed beach bar having a drink. 'Nothing alcoholic,' William had said. 'Just juice, I guess.' So Nick had a beer and William was drinking chemical bottled orange juice (in the State where citrus fruit grows like weeds), sitting on bar stools on the edge of the sand, served by brown-skinned blonde girls in bikini tops and abbreviated shorts.

'It sounds the sort of life I need.' Nick sighed. 'Perfect simplicity.'

'The Dark world's a maze. In the Sunlight all is made clear. You make your life with us and ... no more problems. That

I guarantee. Will you come to us?' William was still smiling at Nick and looking at him through clear blue eyes with irresistible sincerity.

'If only I could ...'

'Of course you can. Anyone can. Knock and it shall be opened to you.'

'What shall be opened?'

'Home. Our home and your home. The Sun Valley that's waiting for you.'

'I can't imagine a real home,' Nick said in the most desolate voice he could manage. 'I haven't really had a home life for a hell of a long time.'

'We all make our contribution.' William went on smiling at him. 'All we ask of you is your talent. What's your talent, Nicholas?'

'Me? Oh, I'm a teacher.'

'We need teachers. Teachers will help us educate the world in happiness and positive thinking.'

'What else do you need?'

'All sorts: builders, carpenters, cooks, doctors.'

'Economists?' Nick made an informed guess, based on the letter from me that he had by now received.

'We have the best. We had a bad experience in that department, but now we have the very best. One of our most zealous children.'

'I wonder who ...' Nick began to ask, but William gave him another welcoming smile and put a hand gently on his arm.

'No more questions, Nicholas. I'm not questioning you about your life or whatever it is that's making you live in Darkness. Come to us in Sunshine. Save the questions until you're safe inside the family.'

'What's *your* work exactly?' Nick asked William.

'My work, Nicholas, is to bring back friends.'

'Bring them back where?'

'Home. You've got your Volks, haven't you. What're we waiting for?'

'I must say, I'm interested.'

'I know you are.'

'I'd like to visit you.'

'To visit with us is to stay with us. You won't want to do anything else. Come and see. Once they're home, no one cares to leave Sun Valley.'

'Well.' Nick finished his drink. 'I don't know what I've got to lose.'

'Only the chains of Darkness.' William smiled at him. 'Shall we go? Oh, and you'll find you won't have a need of that stuff any more.' He nodded towards Nick's beer. 'Only fruit juice and the Word of the Master.'

So eventually they drove off in Nick's old Volkswagen, with William talking soothingly all the time, so that with the heat and the gentle voice repeating encouraging sentiments and messages of hope, Nick said that he felt, in a way, hypnotized and almost fell asleep as he drove along the freeway.

In time they turned off at an exit and were driving past fields and orchards, fruit farms and shacks, low-lying country much afflicted by mosquitoes and hurricanes. They drove on for almost an hour, William giving directions and comfort, and my son Nick saying as little as was needed to keep up the pretence of his disillusionment with a harsh world and of his readiness to put his life at the service of an unknown Master and join the Children of Sun.

'Happiness outside is a thing that has to be forced on you, by money or sex or some other kind of hallucinogenic drug. But flowers don't need money to grow, Nick. They don't need the Big Job of the Wonderful Home. It's because they have the warmth of the Sun *inside* them. You're going to see a whole lot of sights where we're going to, Nicholas, and I sure can't wait to show them to you. But one thing you won't see, and that's an unhappy face.'

'What do I have to do? To get in to your home?' Nick asked innocently.

'Just decide to stay.'

'Is that all?'

'Well. If you do decide to stay with us, Nicholas, there is a contract.'

'A legal document?'

'Scarcely. You have to write out the words of power. And write them in rather a special way.'

'Oh, really? And what sort of a special way is that?'

William turned to Nick for a moment and said quietly, 'You write in your own lifeblood, Nicholas. Everyone does. It doesn't take much to do it.'

At last they came to a high wall, running along the side of a narrow country road. And then there was a wide gate in the wall, painted white and topped with barbed wire. Over the gate there was a high, wooden arch and a sign reading SUN VALLEY and high and triumphant over the sign was a large, glass-covered coloured photograph of a cleric, a man with crinkly white hair, kindly eyes beaming behind rimless spectacles and a deep and healthy suntan. Nick didn't recognize the photograph, but then he had never been in Percival Simpson's bed-sit in Alexander Herzen Road.

William asked Nick to stop in front of the gate, and he clasped his hands and raised them towards the photograph. 'The Master,' he said. Then he asked Nick to honk the horn, and a couple of clean-shirted, large and healthy-looking young men came out of the shed by the gate and looked into the car. William rolled down the window and spoke to them.

'A new friend and brother,' he said. 'His name's Nicholas.'

Nick said that the smiles of the gatekeepers seemed to be suddenly switched on like street lights at twilight.

'Be very welcome, Nicholas.'

'May the Sun shine always on a new friend.'

At which one of them unlocked the huge padlock which held the gate, and the other swung it open.

'We're home, Nicholas,' said William. 'Just drive in slowly.'

Nick, bless his heart, drove in for the sake of the defence of Percival Simpson, and he said it was an extremely unpleasant moment when he heard the gates close and the padlock snap behind him.

There was nothing immediately obvious that could explain the distinct sense of foreboding that my son Nicholas Rumpole felt. What he had driven into was like a spacious and very well-kept farmyard. There was a line of sheds where he guessed animals were kept, and another line of buildings on the other side of the square which might have housed offices and communal rooms. The bottom of the square was also blocked by buildings of some sort, so that the compound was effectively closed in, in a way that made Nick think of a well-run open prison. The inhabitants, however, were all much like William, young men and women, wearing clean jeans and smiling. In a corner of the yard a group were loading boxes and sacks of vegetables onto a new pick-up truck. As they worked they were singing:

> 'Gonna build a kingdom on this sad old ground,
> Gonna build a kingdom all around!
> Gonna call it heaven, cause that's what it'll be,
> A place of beauty, joy and peace for you and me!'

'The Sun's Children,' William said. 'We're always singing.' Strangely enough Nick didn't find even this fact reassuring.

At William's instructions he drove across to the row of communal buildings. He parked and they got out. William led him to what seemed to him to have been a converted cowshed and opened a door.

'This is the reception area, Nicholas. Wait in here. Be at peace, and I'll tell the office you've arrived to make your home with us.'

'Well, I'm not sure ...' Nick sounded doubtful, but William said firmly, 'Wait here, Nicholas. The Parents in Love will be here to greet a new child. No further decisions are expected of you.'

William left, and Nick found himself in a long room, furnished with sofas and easy chairs. The walls were decorated with a number of bright but amateurish murals of young men and women and some children, walking naked across a primitive landscape hand in hand, or holding up their arms to a round yellow sun surrounded by spiky rays and painted as it would be in a child's painting. The naked figures were so turned that there was no direct display of their private parts, and indeed their sex wasn't always easy to determine. Almost the whole of an end wall was covered with a hugely blown-up photograph of the beaming cleric whose picture hung over the gateway. Hymn tunes of a cheerful nature were being piped into the room by some mechanical musak system. There were

114

long coffee tables on which stood bowls of flowers. There were no newspapers or magazines, no books and no ashtrays.

Nick went to the long windows and stood looking out into the yard. He saw the industrious young people loading the truck; he could see the guardians of the gate talking together by their shed. And then he saw another group of three or four Sun Children come out of what may have been an office and set off towards the building at the end of the square. They were carrying ledgers and files, and walking a little behind them, as though too tired to keep up, he saw Tiffany Jones.

The door was unlocked, either by good luck or by William's forgetfulness. Nick was out of it in a moment and standing in the sunshine calling, 'Tiffany!'

'Nick! It's you. Have you come inside?'

She stood there, a beautiful black girl with her arms full of files, half turned towards him, and he could hear the exhaustion in her voice, although it was denied by the bright and perpetual smile worn by all the Children of Sun.

'Tiffany. What are you doing? We all missed you. Paul's gone crazy looking for you.'

'I'm working, Nick. Working for the Master.' She looked round nervously and lowered her voice. 'We're not supposed to talk ... Not to Outside People.'

'Working? What the hell are you working at?'

'Oh, the books. Using my skill in figures. I work so hard, Nick.'

'Tiffany. Tell me.' Nick asked what I needed to know.

'I can't tell you. The last guy they had ... for accounting ... He was a traitor! He betrayed them, you see? That's why they needed me.'

'Who was he, Tiffany?'

She didn't answer his question and Nick looked round; one of the young men from the gate was coming towards them. 'I can't stop. We'll meet and talk. Not one to one, however. We can only talk together. With all the Children ...'

On the other side of the square the loading of the pick-up truck was finished, the driver was climbing into his seat and the crowd of loaders was moving away towards the large building at the end. The young man from the gate was moving towards Nick, calling out to him in a voice which had lost some degree of warmth.

'Hey! Hey, you friend. Is that your Volks?'

'Be welcome, Nick. Be very welcome,' Tiffany said faintly.

As she moved away from him, Nick was looking at the cardboard-covered file which was top of those in the black girl's arms. There was a name written on the cover, which had been crossed out, the name 'Percival'.

'Drive that up to the car port with the other gifts.' The young man instructed Nick in a voice that made it clear that it was less a request than an order. Nick looked to the open shed at which the young man was pointing, in which stood a number of new, and not so new, motor cars. Then he pulled his car door open.

'Tiffany.' He spoke to her as calmly as he could. 'Let me take you home.'

'Don't be ridiculous, Nick.' She was smiling at him, and at that moment her smile seemed particularly weary. 'I am home.'

It was the last he saw of her.

'Come on, friend. Move, why don't you?'

The young man from the gatehouse was not to be denied. Nick swung into the driving seat and saw through his dusty windscreen that the gate was open wide to let the truck full of vegetables out. He switched on his engine, put his foot flat on the floor and gripped the steering wheel as his car shot forward. He reached the gate in a cloud of dust just as the truck was moving through it, and, ignoring the shouts of the gatekeepers, he managed to get through in the truck's wake before the gate could close behind it. There was a space in front of the gate in which Nick could pass the truck, and then a long narrow road between banks where he tried to get away from the truck, but it accelerated also and seemed near enough to touch his back bumper.

Then the road twisted and Nick saw the lumbering back of a slow-moving harvester in front of them. He twisted his wheel and, half mounting the bank, managed to squeeze his little Volkswagen past the agricultural implement, leaving the vegetable truck stuck closely behind it. Nick didn't lift his foot from the floor when he reached the freeway, but though he watched his mirror no one seemed to be giving him chase. He didn't feel safe, however, until he had parked in front of his house, got inside and poured himself a long, cold glass of Californian white wine in the cause of freedom. He then lifted the telephone and put in a call to Equity Court in the Temple.

Chapter Fifteen

'Splendid, Nick. Absolutely splendid. My dear boy, I'm grateful. What a sad loss you are to the law! Well, of course your mother's all right. What on earth's she got not to be all right about? Well, that's very kind ... I miss you too, Nick. Of course I do.'

As I put down the instrument, I became aware of the presence of Guthrie Featherstone lurking by my desk.

'Rumpole! I really think it's time I had a word.'

'That son of mine,' I said in some elation, 'is a chip off the old block, Featherstone. He's just done a splendid job on the Simpson murder case. An absolutely splendid job.'

'Rumpole. I've been talking things over with Henry and I've come to the conclusion that we've got an overflow problem in Chambers.'

'Then why don't you pull out the plug, my old darling. Do you have to go on finding room for that sinister little Welshman?'

'Glendour-Owen has an excellent practice. But you see, we had made our plans on the clear basis of your retirement.'

'Don't tell me you can't find room for me, Featherstone.' I was in no mood to bandy words with my Head of Chambers. 'I hear you were thinking of taking on another lady, some blonde bombshell who hunts and picks up matrimonials.'

'That was rather different. Elizabeth Chandler could have mucked in with Philly. Anyway, I've rather given up on that idea,' said Featherstone, admitting his total defeat at the hands of the redoubtable Miss Trant.

'Well, then. There's absolutely no problem.'

'Oh yes there is, Rumpole. Look, if you *are* coming back to the Bar, which at your time of life I don't honestly advise, I just think you'll have to make other arrangements.'

I looked at Featherstone then with a sort of pity. The poor fellow had no idea of the gaping pit which was about to open at his feet. 'You can't do it, my old darling,' I said. 'You simply can't afford to lose me, Featherstone. You see, you absolutely rely on me to defend you. On a serious charge, before a quite merciless tribunal.'

'Oh really, Rumpole. And what tribunal are you talking about?'

'I am talking, my dear Featherstone, about your wife Marigold.'

And then I told him about the serious charges laid against him, matters which his wife hadn't seen fit to mention in the privacy of their home, and the embarrassing divorce case she was planning. And as I was the only advocate with the smallest chance of winning him a verdict of not guilty, I pointed out, and he saw the force of the argument, that continued prattle about there being no room for Rumpole in Chambers was a foolish waste of time.

Featherstone sat with his jaw dropped and a glassy look in his eye. He seemed to see the distant vision of Mr Justice Featherstone in scarlet and ermine vanish before his eyes.

'Marigold *can't* have seen me,' he tried to argue hopelessly, 'in the perfume department.'

'She has the evidence of her own eyes,' I assured him. 'I'm afraid she's prepared to believe them.'

'Or in the restaurant?' he added hopefully.

'There the prosecution relies on her brother's testimony.'

'Tom must have been mistaken.'

'Unlikely. And even if he were ...'

'Yes?'

'In view of the nature of the tribunal, I think he's likely to be believed.' As with all clients, it was better to point out the worst of the case to Featherstone. Then he would be more grateful for any small success I might achieve.

'Rumpole. I rely on you.' He looked at me in a beseeching sort of way.

'I know.'

'Marigold simply won't discuss the matter with me. She's hardly spoken for the last ten days.'

'So you want me to defend you?' I appeared to be thinking the matter over.

'Please, Rumpole.' His dependence on me was almost endearing. I have always found it hard to actually dislike my clients, so I gave him the benefit of my advice and experience.

'Nothing's so unconvincing as a bare denial. That's what I told Bertie Timson.'

'Who the hell's Bertie Timson?'

'Oh, just one of my other villains,' I told him casually, at which Featherstone protested.

'Rumpole!'

'The old darling stands accused of carrying house-breaking instruments by night. "Come out with a bare denial", I told Bertie, "and no one believes you." Now if the truth of the matter is that you *were* in the perfume department ...' I brought the general principle back to fit the specific facts in Featherstone *v.* Featherstone.

'But there is some quite innocent explanation!' Featherstone was taking to the life of crime like a duck to water.

'And for you sitting in the restaurant with whoever it was?' I asked.

'Does Marigold *know* who it was?' he asked with terror in his voice, seeing a scandal approaching which would involve the whole of Chambers.

'Not by name. She says she was a floosie. Some little tart from the King's Road,' I reassured him.

'Oh, Rumpole,' Featherstone said in a voice of doom. 'It was Phillida ...'

'Can you possibly mean Miss Phillida Trant, LL.B. (Hons.) of London University, member of this distinguished Chambers?' I asked incredulously, turning the knife in the self-inflicted wound.

'Yes, Rumpole. I'm afraid that's exactly who it was.'

'Then if there *is* an innocent explanation ... ?' I put the situation before him, in all its seriousness. 'You *must* let me come out with it. Otherwise I don't give a toss for your chances, quite frankly.'

'Of course, Rumpole. An entirely innocent explanation,' Featherstone assured me, somewhat desperately.

'We could call Miss Phillida Trant to give evidence. I imagine she's a witness who would carry a good deal of weight, even with the most obstinate tribunal.'

'Well, no.' Featherstone was doubtful. 'No, I don't think we could really ask Phillida.'

As with Bertie Timson, I saw the red light at once. There is no course more fatal to the defence than calling an unhelpful witness. However, I did my best to fill Featherstone with a sense of urgency. 'Your lady wife says she'll be back to speak to me.'

'Tell her, Rumpole!' He was beseeching me now. 'She'll listen to you. I'm *sure* she'll listen.'

'Tell her? Of course I'll tell her. I'll put your case to her. Fair and square. The only problem is, Featherstone, my old darling defendant ...'

'Yes?'

'As yet I have absolutely no idea what your case is.'

There was a long pause and then he said, 'I'll think about it.'

'Well, you'd better think quickly,' I warned him. 'Marigold will be here in exactly a week's time.'

In the interim my instructing solicitor, young Michael Mowbray, visited the village near to which the Hon. Rory Canter had farmed almost a thousand acres of rich and productive Hampshire countryside. He drove up to the farmhouse of mature and sunlit Georgian brick, he admired the newly painted white gates and gleaming farm machinery, he saw how sleek and well the black and white cows appeared to be as they were driven to the milking machines, and how neatly and in what good time the fields were ploughed. He also noticed that such farm workers as he saw looked young and intelligent and quite unlike the usual Hampshire labourer.

Having taken a view of the property, Mowbray had a pint of beer and a plate of bread and cheese in the local pub, The Baptist's Head. There he heard that Fineacre Farm had been taken over by a foreign company, the exact nature of which was unknown to the red-faced, panting landlord, but which seemed to employ a work force of young people who kept themselves a great deal to themselves and were an absolute dead loss as customers. More than that my instructing solicitor could not learn, so he left, having promised to come back at an early date and sample the landlord's Cordon Bleu French dinner, which featured chicken boiled in red wine, frozen vegetables and the Gastronomic Gâteau Trolley – a promise which Mike Mowbray, who despite his deep and long-lasting friendship with Ken Cracknell was a young man of some taste and discernment, had no intention of keeping.

He drove next to the neighbouring town and sought five minutes with the local solicitor, who happened to employ as London agents the firm where Mowbray had served his articles. He said he had a client, and hinted at untold wealth and Arab connections, who was interested in buying the Fineacre property. The elderly partner smiled, shook his head and said he doubted very much if the present owners would sell. He himself had acted in the rather unusual transaction by which they had acquired the farm from Rory Canter. From him Mowbray was able to discover who these owners were, and when he passed the information on to me, I was more eager than ever for the date of the Simpson trial, and to pass on the facts I had collected to an Old Bailey jury.

'In my humble submission to the Court ... I'm sorry, I mean to you, Mrs Featherstone ... you have absolutely no reason for a divorce, or indeed to feel any emotion except ... conjugal love ... and gratitude towards my client. I mean your husband.'

Before tackling the problems of Percival Simpson, I had Guthrie Featherstone's defence to take care of, and I was engaged on pleading his cause, based on the new and ingenious set of instructions he had given me after our preliminary conference. As I opened the proceedings I saw the tribunal looking distinctly frosty. It was as I had feared all along: Mrs Marigold Featherstone was going to prove a hard nut to crack, and she was as unsmiling as a Methodist Magistrate faced with a bad case of flashing in Chapel.

'What should I say? "Thank you very much, Guthrie, for messing about with a floosie"?'

'And on that charge I shall be able to demonstrate that Guthrie Featherstone, Q.C., M.P., is entirely innocent,' I assured the Court.

'Innocent!' The voice of Marigold Featherstone was the voice of scorn.

'Oh yes. All men are innocent until they're proven guilty.' I thought I'd better remind her of the proud principle of British justice.

'Well, he is "proven guilty", as you call it, by the evidence of my own eyes. And of Tom's eyes.'

You see what she was like? She was of the stuff of which Judge Bullingham was made, with his talent for taking every possible point against the defence.

I came in from another angle and said quietly, 'Mrs Featherstone. When is your wedding anniversary?'

'Next month. The twenty-first. Guthrie always forgets it.'

'Well, this year he didn't forget it. He remembered it, most devotedly. Tell me, Mrs Featherstone, do you like "Ma Tendresse" perfume?'

I could see the question had surprised her, but she answered impatiently, 'I have absolutely no idea. I have never tried it.'

'Then it will be a new experience. Your husband hopes you'll find it enjoyable,' I told her quietly.

'What on earth do you mean?'

'He went into Harrods to buy you a large bottle of "Ma Tendresse" as a present for your wedding day.'

The Court thought this over, appeared to reflect, but then said, with a first appearance of doubt, 'But Tom saw him in the restaurant ...'

'Purely circumstantial evidence,' I assured her hastily. 'On which so many people have been wrongly convicted.'

'You're not suggesting Tom was mistaken?' The Court was still hostile, although perhaps less determined.

'Not in what he saw,' I said reasonably, 'but in the *interpretation* to be placed upon it. You see, Guthrie had just slipped into the Trattoria ... and he happened to see a lady, a member of the Bar as a matter of fact, waiting for a girl-friend.'

'A member of the Bar?' Obviously she hadn't even considered the possibility.

'Oh yes, Mrs Featherstone. A profession open to all sorts and conditions of men and women. He sat down to chat to her, about a case they were involved in, a long firm fraud.'

'Fraud indeed!' Marigold was her old scornful self.

'And then he left her.' I ignored the interruption. 'Her friend never turned up and she went shortly afterwards.'

'But they opened a parcel. A bottle of scent.' I could see that the Court was shaken.

'Of course! He wanted her opinion, as a woman rather than a lawyer, on his choice of a present for you.'

'Oh really? And why did he happen to slip into the Trattoria Gallactica?'

I allowed a long pause and then smiled and said softly, 'Can't you guess?'

'I certainly can't.'

It was time to play my last trump. If this didn't work, then nothing would. 'He went in to book a table, of course. It is there he intends to take you out for a slap-up spread, Mrs Featherstone, with champagne laid on regardless, to celebrate a decade of happy marriage. On the twenty-first of next month!'

After the hard hour with Mrs Featherstone, I went to meet Guthrie, by arrangement, in Pommeroy's Wine Bar where he was waiting for me with considerable anxiety. In fact he could hardly bring himself to ask, 'Rumpole! How did it go?'

'I think I can say, Featherstone, that it was touch and go until my final speech,' I told him, after I had settled down and forced him to buy a bottle of the Pichon Longueville, Pommeroy's best and most costly wine.

'What did you say?'

'I reminded the Court that she enjoyed considerable status as your wife. In the course of time she would almost certainly become Lady Marigold, when you are elevated to the High Court Bench. I think that tipped the scales.'

'And the result was?' Featherstone was looking at me in a hunted fashion. I took a long gulp and reassured the poor blighter.

'I would say, a conditional discharge. "Tell Guthrie I'll forget the divorce," she said, "if he puts his back into being made a judge." '

'Oh, thank God! I say, that's splendid, Rumpole! Of course I owe it to Marigold to get my bottom on the High Court Bench eventually.'

'I think you do.' I regarded him judicially and said, 'I think you've got off extremely lightly, I must say.'

'Well, yes.' At least he admitted it.

'At the mere cost of a bottle of French pong, a slap-up do at the Eyetie restaurant, and a dozen of the Pichon Longueville.'

'A dozen?'

'Or should we say two dozen? Twenty-four is a good round number and the advocate, as you always say, my old darling, is worthy of his hire. Oh, by the way, Featherstone. I hear you've been taken in to prosecute Bertie Timson on a quite ridiculous charge of being in possession of house-breaking implements by night, and complicity in the Steadfast Savings Bank robbery. You will remember, won't you, that there may always be an innocent explanation, however unlikely it may sound? Oh, and Guthrie ...'

'Yes, Horace?' Featherstone sounded more friendly than at any time since my return.

'About my leaving Chambers ...'

'Well, that's not necessary, of course. Not,' he added, still a little hopefully, 'until you *really* want to retire.'

I was delighted that I had got the old fathead to see reason at last. 'I mean,' I said, 'I must be here in case you need defending again. I seem to have got the ear of Mrs Marigold Featherstone.'

'Oh, you have, Horace, indeed you have! And I'm most grateful for it.'

I don't know if Guthrie bore my words in mind, but he prosecuted Bertie Timson like a gentleman. In due course I got my two dozen of Pommeroy's very best and Bertie got acquitted, for which he said a profound and heartfelt *merci beaucoup*. I approached the opening of the Notting Hill Gate Murder at the Old Bailey, therefore, well lubricated with the best stuff, and with a great deal of my early confidence restored.

Chapter Sixteen

By and large I was satisfied with my preparations for my leading role in the case of R. *v.* Simpson. I had played my cards
pretty close to my chest and I hadn't taken my learned junior,
Ken Cracknell, into my confidence about the nature of the defence. I didn't want him dousing my tender schemes in cold
water just when they had started to take root, and I wanted
to try my ideas out in cross-examination before I paraded them
before anyone. When Ken Cracknell asked me about our
strategy, I would utter such Sibylline phrases as 'I propose
to play it largely by ear', or 'Sufficient unto the day, my dear
fellow', or 'Let's just deny everything and then see where we
go from there'. I had no real time to wonder why, when I made
these hopeless and clearly unprepared pronouncements, my
junior counsel looked far from displeased, but instead gave a
small smile of satisfaction.

One front on which I was making absolutely no progress whatever was in my relations with my client. When I went to see Percival Simpson, as I did on a number of occasions, the last one
being the afternoon before the trial started, he appeared increasingly lethargic and detached from the reality which faced him.

'Look, Duchess,' I protested on that final afternoon, 'you
may not give a toss about the outcome of this case, but it's
exceedingly important to me. I've come out of my alleged
retirement to do this murder, and my whole future, such as it
is, depends on it. It may be a matter of complete indifference
to you, but I desperately want to win.'

'You want to win?' Simpson looked at me; something seemed
to amuse him. 'You want to win my case?'

'That, Duchess, is the general idea. That's why I've been
calling on you religiously over the last few months.'

'Win?' He laughed a little contemptuously.

'That's the ticket.'

'You might as well hope to stop the sun rising tomorrow, or put an end to the tides.'

'What *do* you mean? There's no law of nature which says you have to be found guilty.'

'Don't you think there is?'

'When,' I asked him directly for the umpteenth time, 'are you going to tell me exactly what happened when you went for your holiday in Florida?'

'There's absolutely no point in your asking me questions like that.' Simpson shook his head firmly. 'No point whatsoever.'

'But if I don't ask you questions, how do you expect me to win, Duchess?'

'I don't expect you to win. It's only you who keeps talking about winning.'

Discouraging, I'm sure you'll agree. But in spite of the distinct lack of cooperation from the client, I was in a high and even optimistic frame of mind when Henry said, and I thought I detected a new note of respect in his voice, 'Your murder's in tomorrow, Mr Rumpole. You've got a clean start at 10.30. Court Number Two down the Old Bailey.'

Court Number Two wasn't Court Number One. It was not the absolute centre, not quite the *crème de la crème* of Old Bailey Courts. The great classic murders had taken place in Court Number One. But Number Two was a large and impressive arena, one of the Courts in the old block which opened onto the fine marble-tiled hall with its Edwardian civic murals and statues of judges, away from the liverish-looking pale woodwork and concealed lighting of the new Courts. Number Two Court was home.

As, of course, were all the places I visited that morning went I went down to the Old Bailey to do my poor best, in so far as he would allow me, for the accursed Percival Simpson.

> 'Nor for my peace will I go far,
> As wanderers do, that still do roam;
> But make my strengths, such as they are,
> Here in my bosom, and at home.'

It was ridiculous, but home was walking down to Ludgate Circus in the rain; home was the admirable scrambled eggs produced by the Italian cook in Rex's Café, eaten among the Fleet Street printers who had been up all night, and the early working officers in charge of the case, and a couple of nervous villains, and some over-eager jurors. Home was the Old Bailey entrance, with the friends and relations of various villains reading the list of cases to be tried; home was being greeted by the large officers inside the swing doors; home was going up to the robing room and climbing into the fancy dress. In all this excitement, and drunk with nostalgia, I failed to ask my learned junior, Kenneth Cracknell, Esq., who appeared wearing a lightish-grey suit under his gown (no doubt in some radical protest against the regulation subfusc) with dark hair flowing in some profusion from under his wig, who was the learned Judge whom Fate had selected to preside over the trial of the unhappy Revenue official.

When he told me, I felt a sinking stomach and rising nausea. My hands started to sweat and I was breathing with difficulty. Home, I discovered with something akin to horror, was his Honour Judge Bullingham.

This may need a word of explanation, in case it should seem to the instructed reader that the powers that be, at the Lord Chancellor's office, had taken complete leave of their senses and elevated the crazy Bull to the status of High Court or 'Red' Judges who usually try murders. No such promotion would have been known to history since the day when the late Emperor Caligula made his horse a Consul; and Bullingham remained, at the height of his appalling career, a mere Old Bailey Judge. However, he was an Old Bailey Judge of such seniority that he had been empowered to try murders. Of the two High Court Judges down at the Old Bailey that morning, one was engaged in trying a well-known politician for forgery, and the other was doing something mysteriously connected with the three or four Official Secrets still left to us.

So I drew Judge Bullingham for the eleventh time of asking, and I had the horrible certainty that the old enemy would organize an eleventh crushing defeat, which would make this much sought-after murder the absolute end of the line for Rumpole. If the gods really wish to destroy a person, I remembered, they grant his foolish requests. Had my feverish pursuit of the brief in R. *v*. Simpson been no more than a final act of legal suicide? Filled with such unworthy fears, I kept my eyes to the ground as we all stood and the Bull charged into Court.

But then I remembered that I was an advocate not without experience, that I was doing an important murder that was bound to find its way into the evening papers and would, in all probability, make the *News of the World*, and that the case would not be tried by judge alone, but by a jury of good men, women and teenagers and true who were even then filing into their box in answer to their names. So I took in several deep breaths and accepted, on behalf of defence counsel, the hard luck of the draw. I forced myself to raise my head and look Judge Bullingham in the eye.

Such time as had elapsed since our last encounter had not improved the old devil, and such changes as had taken place might generally be said to have been for the worse. The wig that sat askew his shining bald head seemed even greyer, his yellowing collar and bands looked more grubby and his nose appeared a deeper shade of purple. His eyes had become distinctly more bloodshot, and the lids hung heavily upon them so that they seemed in constant danger of closing, even during the prosecution case when he did his best to appear awake. His teeth, when he opened his mouth to lick the end of his pencil, seemed to be more yellow, and I wondered at what precise moment of the proceedings he would choose to pick his nose, or explore, with an extended little finger, his inner ear.

Our eyes met and he registered, I was pleased to see, the same surprise and dismay that I had felt when I realized that it had been decreed that we should, yet again, work together. Apparently he told his clerk that he thought I'd been put out to grass. He should have known that you can't get rid of Rumpole so easily.

'Mister Rumpole.' The growl came, as usual, somewhere from the depths of the Bull. 'Do *you* appear for the defence?'

When I realized quite clearly that the Judge was just as displeased to see me as I was to be before him, my fear evaporated. I smiled charmingly and gave an inscrutable bow in which I hoped he might have been aware of some small element of mockery.

'Yes, my Lord. I have the honour to represent Mr Percival Simpson. And may I take this opportunity of saying what a pleasure it is to be appearing before your Lordship once again.'

At which the Bull frowned and grunted unhappily. 'Very well,' he said. 'Let's get on with it. Mr Colefax?'

'If your Lordship pleases.' Moreton Colefax, Q.C., leading counsel for the Crown, was a handsome, ex-Guards officer, ex-Eton and New College, member of White's and the Beefsteak Club and a Bencher of his Inn. He was a decent enough prosecutor according to his lights, and I gave him the credit of finding the judicial antics of the Bull, although all meant to assist the prosecution, vulgar and distasteful. I had known Colefax when he was in rompers, doing 'dangerous drivings' in a superior sort of way round the Thames Magistrates Court. He was a man I believed to be totally ignorant on the subject of blood.

'The defence is represented,' Colefax started quietly, 'by my learned friends Mr Horace Rumpole and Mr Kenneth Cracknell. Members of the jury, this case concerns the knifing of a perfectly respectable citizen, a member of a well-known family, late one evening last January in the Notting Hill Gate underground station. It's a somewhat squalid story. '

Oh dear. Poor old Colefax sounded as though the Notting Hill Gate Murder was something he wouldn't wish to touch with a pair of silver sugar-tongs.

'Squalid motives have been suggested for this killing,' Colefax said with some contempt, and I knew that he was referring to the 'Guardsman's Defence' suggested by Ken Cracknell in his cross-examination in the Magistrates Court, which never had a hope. 'Those suggested motives may well be that there was some kind of sexual, or homosexual, reason for this crime. Members of the jury, you will hear that the Honourable Roderick, known as Rory, Canter was a perfectly normal young man sexually, who had as his fiancée a young lady with good family connections and who was himself a young man of strong religious views.'

I smiled at this and made my first note. Colefax had called the deceased 'religious' and there, I thought, the old darling might be on to something.

My nerves were quite settled before I started to cross-examine the Crown's first witness, Mr Byron MacDonald, the guard of the train that had been standing at the platform of Notting Hill Gate station when the Hon. Rory Canter came down the stairs. His evidence, as elicited in its full details by Moreton Colefax, was in no way helpful to the defence. For a start he made it clear that Canter came down to the platform first and was followed by Simpson, who clearly appeared to be the pursuer, whereas Canter was obviously the victim. He saw, he said, Simpson come down, peer about him and then move towards Canter; they were then locked in the struggle which he saw as his train moved away – a chain of events which, there was no possibility of dispute, ended shortly afterwards with the death of Canter.

Now I rose to question the tall Jamaican guard who stood in the witness box in his London Transport uniform. He had been an excellent witness, and I started with the soft touch, the approach courteous and the questions devious.

'Mr MacDonald,' I began. 'You say you saw the deceased, Mr Canter, come on to the platform first?'

'Yes, Mr Rumpole. He said that,' the Judge growled from his notebook.

'And you saw my client, Mr Simpson, come down afterwards?' I went on, ignoring the Bull for the moment.

'Following him, Rumpole. Your client was clearly the pursuer. Going after his victim.'

'No, my Lord. He didn't say "following".' I sounded patient, as if I only wanted to help the Bull, and I picked up the notebook in which my junior had been writing down the evidence. 'I have my learned friend Mr Cracknell's note. The witness said, "He came down afterwards".'

'Well, if you think it makes the slightest difference ...' The Bull snorted and practically winked at the jury as though to say, 'We don't, do we, ladies and gentlemen. We're far too bright to split hairs with the defending barrister.'

'The difference it makes will become apparent by the end of this case. Even to your Lordship.' I must say I was starting to lose my patience with the Bull. He gave a warning growl of 'Mr Rumpole', but I moved rapidly on to the next question before he could give voice to his protest.

'For all you knew the Honourable Rory Canter may have been going down the tube station to *look* for Mr Simpson?'

'I don't know anything about the two gentlemen,' said Mr MacDonald.

'Exactly!' I did my best to sound satisfied with his answer. 'Or if Canter knew that Mr Simpson was about to make that journey, he may have deliberately got to the platform first, to lie in wait for him?'

'That hardly sounds likely, though, does it, Mr MacDonald?' The Judge, falling into his well-loved role as counsel for the prosecution, had put the question.

'My Lord, the witness has already said he didn't know anything about the gentlemen,' I reminded him.

'Then it was quite pointless putting the question, wasn't it, Mr Rumpole?' I got a grin from the yellow teeth, as did the jury.

'I put the question, my Lord, in order that the jury may be aware of all the possibilities.' I did my best to remain polite.

'All the possibilities, Mr Rumpole? However remote?' The jury got another sympathetic smile; the Bull was clearly sorry that they were being troubled by the idiot Rumpole.

'My Lord, indeed yes ...'

'It's hardly likely, is it, that a man would go down to a station platform to wait for his murderer. Or go out looking for the man who's going to attack him?'

'My Lord, I should say that frequently happens.' After all, I had come half way round the world to find Judge Bullingham.

'Very well. Let's get on with it.' The Judge had decided that there was nothing to be gained for the moment from bandying words with Rumpole.

'But you did see the deceased, Canter, waiting in an alcove on the station?' I resumed my dialogue with the witness.

'Yes. He was just standing there,' Mr Byron MacDonald agreed.

'He made no attempt to get on the train?'

'He didn't get on it. No, sir.'

'Although the doors were open, and the train was waiting for him?'

'Yes, it was.'

'So he was clearly waiting for something else.'

'Mr Rumpole. How can the witness tell that?' The Judge came back into the arena.

'He stood there, waiting to accost my client, Mr Simpson, didn't he?' I put the question to the witness, but the Bull growled back.

'I suppose by "accost" you mean "sex", Mr Rumpole.'

'Your Lordship mustn't jump to conclusions, however sensational,' I said politely, although I knew from past experience that the Bull had a resolutely filthy mind.

'Oh, really? I thought we were to be treated to the "Guardsman's Defence".' Bullingham smiled at Colefax this time, with overacted cynicism.

'Your Lordship has the better of me. Is that a legal or a military expression?' I asked innocently, and played straight into the Judge's hands.

'You should know, Mr Rumpole. I've no doubt you've made use of it in a number of cases, when you were practising regularly in this Court.'

When I was practising regularly? What did the old darling think I was doing now? Playing tiddly-winks? I hoped for a normal and uninterrupted cross-examination and turned again to the witness. 'Mr MacDonald, you did see Mr Canter move forward and speak to Mr Simpson, my client?'

'I think I did see that, yes.'

That was something, and at least the Bull was quiet. I had another fact to establish.

'And tell me, Mr MacDonald. How long would it be before the next train arrived?'

'I think about five minutes.'

'My last question. You never saw my client produce any sort of a knife?'

'No.'

'He never saw any knives at all, because his train left the station!' Bullingham reminded the jury triumphantly.

And then, as I sat down with my work on Mr Byron MacDonald completed, the Judge sighed with relief and asked Moreton Colefax the name of his next witness.

'Revere, my Lord. Miss Diana Revere.'

If any members of the jury had found their attention wandering during my cross-examination of Byron MacDonald, they were clearly riveted by Miss Diana 'Smokey' Revere. She came into the witness box wearing tight black leather with her orange hair stuck out like the quills of a hedgehog, her eyes were shadowed black and her lipstick and fingernails a shade of mauve. She was chewing gum and as she walked she rattled, from the chains she wore round her neck, like a spectre. The Bull looked at her with his eyes bulging, as though years of whisky had finally destroyed the last of his brain cells and he was gently hallucinating.

'Are you Miss Diana Revere?' Moreton Colefax seemed to have some difficulty in bringing himself to speak to her. She was, in fact, a beautiful although strangely dressed eighteen-year-old girl, who would never have crossed the path of the prosecution Q.C. except in a courtroom.

'They calls me Smokey.' Miss Revere was actually smiling at the Bull, but he looked severely shaken and said, 'Well, never mind about that. Let's get on with it.'

'Miss Revere, were you going down Notting Hill Gate underground station on the night of Thursday, March the 13th?'

'Yeah. With my friends. We were on our way to see the "Public Execution" at Watford.'

'Do they still have those at Watford?' the Bull asked, and the jury laughed obediently.

'No. The "Public Execution". It's a group, innit? Great sound,' Diana explained patiently, as though to a child.

'Did you notice anything on the platform?'

'Yeah, I saw the two geezers.'

Moreton Colefax, who had noticed that Smokey's evidence

seemed to be fighting its way past some impediment said, 'Miss Revere. Are you eating something?'

'Sorry, my Lord.' Smokey smiled politely, removed her chewing gum with a slender finger and stuck it under the ledge of the witness box.

'What were the two men doing?'

'Well. One was sat on the seat. The other, him what had the bag from the take-away ...'

'Which one had the bag from the Delectable Drumstick chicken shop?'

'My Lord, there's no dispute that that was my client, Mr Simpson,' I said, I thought helpfully.

'No, Mr Rumpole! I imagine there can be no possible dispute about that.' The Bull growled; he was a person who was incapable of simple gratitude.

'Yes, Miss Revere. We can take it that the man with the bag from the chicken shop was Mr Simpson. What happened then?' Moreton Colefax asked.

'Well, we all got into the train. The boys was kicking a tin and they kicked it into the carriage. We saw the geezer with the carrier bag get in the carriage too.'

'You saw Simpson?'

'He sat down the other end. On his own, like.'

'But it was the same carriage?'

'Yes.'

'Miss Revere. Let me ask you this.' An important question was coming, and Moreton Colefax brought himself to smile at the ornate girl in the witness box. 'Did you notice the man on the seat as your train was pulling out of the station?'

'I saw him, yes. On the platform. I was looking out through the glass of the door, I reckon it was. And I saw him topple over.'

'He toppled over?' Colefax repeated, and the jury were listening interestedly.

'Sort of slid sideways, like. Went all limp and boneless.'

'Why did you think that was?' the Bull asked her.

'I thought maybe he was pissed, or had a bit of the needle. You get a lot of those, round Notting Hill tube.'

'You mean he was drunk?' Moreton Colefax translated.

'How did you guess?' Miss Revere said, and the usher called 'Silence!' before the jury could laugh.

'Did you happen to notice Mr Simpson sitting at the end of your carriage?'

'I just remember him. He was looking in his plastic bag, like. And then I looked away and I think he dropped something into it. I don't know what it was. I heard it drop in. Something heavy, and metal, I think.'

'What did he do then?'

'He closed his eyes and leant back. It looked like he wanted to go to sleep.'

The strange-looking girl and her dramatic evidence had a powerful effect on the jury. I rose to try and neutralize the damage.

'Miss Revere. When you got down to the platform, a train was just coming in?'

'Yes.'

'So that it must have been about five minutes after the previous train left.'

'I don't know about that.'

'How *can* she know?' the Bull grumbled.

'Very well. Miss Revere, I don't suppose you noticed my client particularly at this time?'

'Not particularly, no.'

'So you can't be certain about what you saw him do.'

'I heard about the murder the next day. It came on the telly. Then I remembered what I'd seen.'

'You say you saw my client close his eyes, as though he were tired.'

'He looked like it. Yes.'

'You may know that it's a common reaction to be exhausted after you've made a violent attack?' Bullingham asked Smokey. He was absolutely ruthless.

'I suppose so.' Smokey looked suddenly bored, anxious to end her time in the witness box. I had no reason to keep her there except to ask, 'And you may also know that people are frequently exhausted and in a state of violent shock after they've *been* attacked?'

'Yeah. I think so.'

'And you didn't see him writing at all?' I asked very loudly and before the Bull could get a word in edgeways. 'You didn't see my client writing on any sort of scrap of paper?'

'No, I didn't.'

'Thank you, Miss Revere,' I said, and sat down and stared with mysterious triumph at the jury.

After the excitement provided by Diana Smokey Revere, there came a dullish afternoon of agreed evidence, police photographers, map-drawers, fingerprint experts, ambulance men and the like, and after Court Ken Cracknell met Miss Trant for a drink in Pommeroy's and a discussion of Rumpole's first day on the murder.

'The Judge is firing all his guns at the defence, and the prosecution witnesses are lethal,' Ken told Phillida, and she smiled and said, 'Then Rumpole must be in his element.'

'I'm not so sure. He was looking a bit grey round the edges at the end of the day.'

'No, he's enjoying it,' Miss Trant was certain, and on the whole she was right. 'As for you, Ken' – she looked at her radical admirer with soft-eyed devotion and put her hand on his across their plonk-stained table at Pommeroy's – 'you're angelic to have wangled this brief for Rumpole. It's just what he needs.'

'I hope so,' Ken said and smiled a little. 'I very much hope it'll do the trick.'

'Claude's going away to stay with his parents next week. He's taking the baby. I can't get away to go with them. It's this long robbery I'm in.'

'What a pity.' Ken was smiling.

'Yes, isn't it. We might have that hamburger you're always on about.'

'And you might see where I live. It's actually perfectly comfortable.'

'I'm sure,' said Miss Trant and her eyes were, I believe, full of promise. 'I'm absolutely sure it is.'

And much later I was in my shirt sleeves working out a way to cross-examine Detective Inspector Wargrave, the officer in charge of the case, and Hilda was knitting some kind of bala-clava helmet or other comfort for the new generation of Rumpoles, when she suddenly asked me, most unusually, how I had got on at Court.

'Bloody badly,' I told her frankly. 'The client won't talk to me and the Bull's madder than ever. I wonder what I'd get, for doing a judge grievous bodily harm?'

Hilda clicked her tongue, worked with her knitting needles and then said, 'That's what you came back to, Rumpole!'

'Don't tell me.'

'I will tell you. I know now. It wasn't even another woman! You came back because you care more for Judge Bullingham than you do for me.' She looked at me in an accusing manner, and I smiled and answered, as I thought, reasonably.

'If you think that, Hilda, wouldn't you really be happier back on the other side of the Atlantic?'

She looked at me in silence for a while, and then she said enigmatically, 'I'm really not sure, Rumpole. But I shall have to think about it.'

I looked at her then, with a sort of vague stirring of hope that perhaps in the not too distant future my freedom would return.

Chapter Seventeen

The first witness the next morning was the Honourable Rory Canter's elder brother, Lord Freith. He was a man in his early forties, quite at his ease in the witness box, and he and Moreton Colefax talked to each other as if they were members of the same club, which indeed they were. The learned judge listened obsequiously, as though he were the slightly comic butler, and the jury and defence counsel were also allowed to overhear.

'Lord Freith,' Moreton Colefax allowed himself to touch an unpleasant subject, 'had your younger brother, to your knowledge, any homosexual tendencies?'

'I can honestly say, my Lord,' Lord Freith included the Bull in the chat, in a truly democratic manner, 'that he had absolutely none.'

'Absolutely none.' Bullingham wrote the words down obediently.

'I think he was of a serious, indeed a religious disposition.'

'He was extremely religious. And, I'm sure, sincerely so.'

'Your brother Roderick, I think,' Colefax continued, 'had a fiancée and was engaged to be married?'

'Oh yes. They'd both dined with me that night at my club. There was absolutely none of the Oscar Wildes about Rory.'

'Thank you, Lord Freith.' Colefax sat down gracefully, with every sign of satisfaction.

I got a dirty look from the Judge. 'I suppose you've got some questions, Mr Rumpole?' he said.

'Just a few. Lord Freith,' I said, rising to my feet, 'your club is where?'

'In St James's.'

'And after dinner did Rory drive his fiancée home?'

'To her flat in Chelsea,' Lord Freith agreed.

'And *he* lived in Eaton Square?'

'Eaton Place, actually.'

'Another address in south-west London?'

'Yes ...' Lord Freith frowned as if wondering where these questions were leading.

'Have you any idea what he was doing north-west? In Notting Hill Gate?'

'No. As a matter of fact,' Lord Freith agreed, 'I've wondered about that.'

'So have I. So may the jury. It was nowhere near his route, was it, from St James's to Chelsea?'

'No,' Lord Freith admitted.

'Or from Chelsea to Eaton Place?'

'No ...'

Things were going too well for the Bull not to intervene. Accordingly he bared his teeth and said menacingly, 'Mr Rumpole. If you're suggesting that this gentleman's brother went to Notting Hill Gate for immoral purposes, I think you should put it fair and square.'

I decided to put an instant stop to this line of judicial offence and I decided to say, 'My Lord, although I'm well aware that a dirty mind is a perpetual feast, I'm making absolutely no such suggestion.'

It was a minor hit. There was laughter in Court, in which Judge Bullingham did not join. He merely grumbled, 'I'm glad to hear it,' being, in fact, quite clearly disappointed.

I turned to Lord Freith and another topic. 'You've told us that your late brother was of a sincerely religious disposition.'

'He's told us that,' the Bull grumbled and only just forgot to add, 'Let's get on with it.'

'And you didn't entirely approve of his religious views, did you, Lord Freith?'

'I didn't approve of all he did, no,' the witness answered carefully.

'Had he made over his farm in Hampshire, by way of a gift, to the particular religious sect he favoured?'

Lord Freith hesitated and then answered frankly, 'He had. He was merely staying on as a manager.'

'Had he also given them a great deal of money?'

'I believe he had.'

'All the money he inherited from your father?'

'I think most of it.'

'And was his fiancée of the same religious persuasion?'

'Yes. They'd met when Rory was in Florida, playing polo. I believe she converted him.'

'So he gave all he had to the poor?'

'We have pretty good authority for *that*, Mr Rumpole.' Bullingham, that great man of religion, was looking wisely at the jury, and some of them even did me the disservice of nodding solemnly and assuming serious and devout expressions.

When I asked my next rude question it was a bit like belching in church. 'Except that you thought he'd given all he had to the rich. You believed it was an extremely rich organization, didn't you, Lord Freith?'

To my great relief the witness seemed to agree with me. 'I thought perhaps they were exploiting Rory,' he said, choosing his words with care.

At the moment when it appeared that I was winning the witness over to my still obscure purposes, Moreton Colefax rose to make a gentlemanly interruption. 'Perhaps my learned friend would be good enough to tell us the name of this alleged organization ...'

'Oh, doesn't my learned friend know it?' I carefully simulated amazement. 'The name is to be found on that blood-stained scrap of paper, the prosecution's Exhibit One.' I held out my hand and the usher got it for me. 'Thank you, usher. It reads "Sunlight Children of Sun". They call themselves "The Children of Sun", don't they, Lord Freith?'

We had the jury's undoubted interest as he answered, 'I believe that's what they're called.'

'And they offer "Blood to Children of Dark".'

'We've been told that the document was written by your client in the deceased's blood, Mr Rumpole.' Bullingham was beginning to feel out of his depth and so, as usual, he attacked the defence.

'My Lord, there hasn't been a scrap of evidence about it,' I told him, feeling the jury watching me closely.

'Mr Moreton Colefax has told us that he's calling Professor

Ackerman. No one knows more about blood stains than Professor Andrew Ackerman.' Bullingham gave the jury a glowing trailer for a prosecution witness.

'I think your Lordship may find that somebody does,' I said, with a certain amount of quiet confidence.

'That would surprise me, Mr Rumpole.'

'Life in your Lordship's Court is full of surprises. I suppose that's why some of us find it so enormously enjoyable.'

Some of the jury appeared to enjoy this, so Bullingham resumed his impatient growl. 'Have you got any more questions for Lord Freith? This must be a painful experience for him.'

It wasn't exactly a Sunday School treat for my client either, I thought. And then I asked the usher for Exhibit Two. I was handed, carefully labelled and wrapped in plastic, the long commando-type sheath knife that had been found inside Simpson's bag of fried chicken. I unwrapped it and examined it carefully in full view of the jury. Then, after a pause long enough to create a suitable tension and feeling of expectancy, I turned to the witness.

'Lord Freith. Your brother went to Sandhurst, I think?'

'Yes, he did.'

'And spent some five years in the army?'

'Yes. Until my father died and left him the farm.'

Lord Freith received the knife from the usher, gave it a cursory glance and put it down on the front of the witness box.

'Do you know that is a regulation army knife, of the sort issued to officers and men undergoing special commando training?'

'I didn't know. But I accept that from you, of course.' Lord Freith was never less than courteous.

'And did your brother, the Honourable Rory Canter, tell you that he had enjoyed such training during his time in the army?'

There was a long pause before the elder brother answered, as casually as possible, 'I believe he told me something of the sort. Yes.'

'Thank you, Lord Freith.' I sat down and glanced at the jury, and I could tell that I hadn't lost their interest.

The learned Judge smiled at Lord Freith with the deepest

respect. 'Thank you, Lord Freith. Your ordeal is over,' he said.
The witness left the box, but our ordeal was continuing.

'What are you up to exactly?' Ken Cracknell whispered to
his learned leader as we were waiting for the next witness to
come into the box. I didn't think he looked particularly elated
by my cross-examination of Lord Freith, which, on the whole,
I would have marked at least eight out of a possible ten.

'Cracknell, perchance you wonder at our show,' I whispered
back at him. 'Then wonder on, till truth makes all things
plain. Who's the next witness?'

'D.I. Wargrave. The officer in charge of the case. At least
you won't be discussing religion with him.' But there, as a
matter of fact, he was mistaken.

After the Detective Inspector had read out, in a monotonous
tone of voice and from his notebook, his account of the police
interview with Simpson, I rose to cross-examine.

'Mr Wargrave, you say that my client told you that he was
guilty?'

'That's what I've got down in my notebook.'

'So, because you've got it down in your notebook, it has the
authority of Holy Writ?'

'Mr Rumpole!' As usual I got the warning growl from the
Bench.

'I suggest he never used the word "guilty" at all. He said he
had "sinned".'

'Doesn't it come to exactly the same thing?' the Judge asked,
and I decided it was time to give him a little basic theology.

'Hardly, my Lord. Every clergyman at morning prayers says,
"I acknowledge my transgressions and my sin is before me."
That can hardly be taken as an admission of stabbing people
down the underground.' I picked up the commando knife and
weighed it in my hand. 'Officer, this knife, Exhibit Two, would
seem to be the fatal weapon.'

'It would seem so, sir.'

'And yet my client possessed a knife, a curved oriental dagger,
which you found on his dressing-table.'

'I did, yes.'

'The jury can see that in the police photograph of my

client's room, next to the blood-stained letter ... photograph number four in your bundle, members of the jury ...' The twelve old darlings leafed through their bundles of photographs and found the place. 'We know there were no blood stains on that dagger.'

'I believe not,' the Detective conceded.

'So it comes to this, does it? My client's knife had not been used, but what had been used was a commando knife of the sort that Mr Canter might have had?'

'*Might* have had. Yes.' D.I. Wargrave sounded dubious as ever.

'And there were two sets of fingerprints on the handle of *that* knife, Exhibit Two ... somewhat blurred. The fingerprints of my client and those of the deceased gentleman.'

'That is so. Yes.'

'And my client's hands were cut and his clothing cut in some places?'

'Yes, indeed.'

'So what does that indicate to you, Inspector?'

'I suppose it might indicate some sort of struggle for the possession of the knife,' Bullingham said, unable to sit quietly and listen to the evidence. The learned Judge had played straight into my hands.

'If your Lordship pleases!' I gave him a low bow in which there was only the faintest touch of mockery. 'Oh, I am extremely grateful to your Lordship. Your Lordship is always the first to appreciate ... points in favour of the defence.'

For a moment Bullingham was speechless, but then he looked at the clock and was saved by it. 'We'll break off now. Shall we say until five past two, members of the jury?' And he added, in a somewhat desperate bid for their favour, 'It may come as a little relief to you, in your consideration of this rather *sordid* case, to know that England are now eighty-five for two in the Test at Melbourne.'

The Judge smiled at them and withdrew. It was a somewhat desperate gambit on his part, and certainly not cricket.

During the luncheon adjournment I took my junior and instructing solicitor down to the cells. There we found the comforting smell of cooking and some screws sitting down to piled plates and great mugs of tea. Our client Simpson came into the little interview room and sat down without a greeting. Young Cracknell, when I looked at him, seemed equally gloomy.

'What's the matter with you all? I get the impression we're doing rather well.' I tried to cheer them up. 'I don't hear anyone say, "The Rumpole hand has lost none of its cunning." I don't hear that exactly.'

'We've still got the letter,' Ken Cracknell sighed. 'You don't write a letter in your victim's blood, not unless it's a deliberate murder. That's what the jury's going to think.'

There was a faint voice: Simpson seemed to be talking to himself. 'The Master is not bound by the laws of man and nature. His is the power of the miraculous.' He then turned to me and said, 'That's what we can't fight. It's no use fighting.'

'You're not going to help me, are you, Duchess? Not until you lose your faith in miracles. Well, that's about to happen,' I told him; it was no use sharing my own doubts and uncertainties with him.

Chapter Eighteen

Professor Andrew Ackerman, that most distinguished patholo-
gist, had been associated with death in its various forms for so
long that he seemed to be ageless. He was a tall, bald man
whose skin had a sort of mortuary pallor and whose voice was
sepulchral and full of respect. He wore small, round, gold-
rimmed spectacles and he gave his evidence impeccably. His
reputation in the Courts was such that he was treated as
infallible by judges and, as the natural successor to the late
Sir Bernard Spilsbury, Ackerman's word on a blood stain, or a
bruise, or a mark of strangulation, was accepted as Holy Writ
down the Bailey. He had only the faintest trace of a Scottish accent from his distant Edinburgh upbringing and he was in fact,
when away from the courtroom or the morgue, a man of
great kindness and quiet humour who spent his holidays bird-
watching and his evenings listening to Baroque music or re-
reading Jane Austen.

'Professor Ackerman. Have you ever tried to write a message
of this sort in blood?'

'For the purposes of this case I did so. It is quite possible,
yes.' The Professor was nothing if not thorough.

'Blood clots in two or three minutes, does it not?' I asked
him.

'Yes, but there would have been continued bleeding from the
deceased in this case.'

'So Mr Simpson would have had to have written this while
he was with the deceased. He couldn't have taken blood home
with him, because it would have clotted?'

'That is so. Yes.'

'The evidence is that he was unobserved on the platform
for about five minutes between the arrival of two trains. He

would have had to write this message during that time, perhaps with the blood on the dagger?'

'It is possible.'

'Just possible, but an extremely strange thing to do?'

'The suggestion is, Mr Rumpole, that you have an extremely strange type of client.' I had left myself wide open to that sort of crack from the Bull.

My mouth was dry and my voice not altogether steady. I took a deep breath, a gulp of water and started a new and entirely friendly dialogue with Professor Ackerman, asking him the questions I had begun to think of, months before, in a Florida library.

'Professor Ackerman, we have known each other for a good many years.'

'Yes, Mr Rumpole, we have.' The mortuary man gave a faint smile.

'And have discussed a good many corpses.'

'Is this to be a time of private reminiscence, Mr Rumpole, or do you intend to cross-examine the Professor?' The Bull was feeling left out of this meeting of old friends. I ignored him.

'And of course the jury may not know as much as you on the subject of blood.' I intended to get down to basics. 'All our red corpuscles are the same.'

'They are. Yes,' Ackerman agreed.

'What varies are the agglutinogens which must fit in with the appropriate agglutinin like a lock fits its own key, and cause the red cells to clump together ... like bunches of grapes?'

'Mr Rumpole. If you and the Professor understand ...' The Bull was restive again. I looked him straight in the eye.

'The system can be made clear,' I said, 'even to the simple mind by saying that those varying types of locks can divide human blood into four groups called, for convenience, "O", "A", "B" and "AB".'

Unlike the Bull, the members of the jury were looking interested, and some of them were taking notes.

'That is exactly so,' Ackerman agreed.

'Class "O" blood is rather common and flows in the veins of forty-five per cent of the population. It flowed in the veins of the Honourable Rory Canter.'

'The deceased was class "O". Yes.'

'Whereas my client, Mr Simpson, is of the forty-one to forty-three per cent whose blood is "A"?'

'He is "A" from the sample I took from him.' The Professor glanced down at his notes.

'And you came to the conclusion that the blood which wrote that letter was class "O" blood, and therefore likely to be Mr Canter's?'

The usher took the exhibit to the Professor, who looked at it again, turning it over with long, surprisingly delicate fingers. 'It responded to the test in that way, yes.'

'You took a minute particle of paper, treated it chemically to detect the antigens and examined it under a microscope?'

'Precisely.'

'Professor Ackerman. When did you think this letter had been written?'

'I assumed, as it was Mr Canter's blood, that it must have been shortly after the murder.'

I gave a small sigh of satisfaction. Ackerman had accepted the instructions given him and, for once, hadn't asked questions.

'But supposing it had been written months before! Suppose my client joined a somewhat dotty religious sect, a sect which required him to write an oath or motto in drops of his *own* blood?'

'But it wasn't his blood group, Mr Rumpole.' Ackerman smiled patiently.

'But if it *had* been, and had been done months before, wouldn't the antigens have perhaps faded in their strength?'

It was the key question, and the Professor considered it. His answer, when it came, was perfectly fair. 'I suppose they might. I hadn't considered that.'

'Consider it now, Professor. I beg of you! The various constituents of blood stains fade in time, don't they?'

'Yes, they do.' He picked up the paper again, with delicate fingers, and looked at it thoughtfully.

'And blood becomes more difficult to classify.'

'I would say, less easy.' Even this caution was good enough for me.

'Less easy! Thank you. But the constituents don't fade evenly, do they? Some factors may vanish before others.'

'It *is* possible.'

'You found my client's blood was "A". Canter's was "O". After that finding you didn't do more tests to break down the classification further?'

'No. The situation seemed perfectly simple.'

'Oh, Professor, let's keep it simple.' I couldn't resist saying, 'For the benefit of the learned Judge.' I went on before there could be any grumbling from the Bench. 'I feel sure the members of the jury will have my point already. Is it not possible that after my client had written this absurd message in his own blood, and kept it, the antigens became less accurately classifiable, and the blood on this paper then gave you an "O" result?'

There was a long pause, during which I hoped I could feel the mystery which surrounded Simpson's defence was beginning to clear. Professor Ackerman picked up the paper again, put it down, smoothed it out and then said, and the words were music to my ears, 'I think the theory you have advanced is a possible one.'

The Bull, of course, was looking disconcerted as he turned to Ackerman. 'Let me get this clear, Professor,' he said, and I hoped he was capable of it. 'Are you saying this letter may have been written by Simpson months before, for some sort of religious reason, in his own blood, and may have nothing to do with this murder?'

'I think now that *may* be so, my Lord.' Ackerman's careful answer was impressive.

'And you can't be sure that it was in fact written in the victim's blood?'

'In view of the possibility that Mr Rumpole has pointed out, no.'

It was then that I silently blessed the good Ackerman and wished him many long and happy years in the morgue.

'Yes, thank you, Professor,' the Bull said, tamed by the Professor's authority. 'I think I understand.'

Wonder of wonders. And I had to hand it to the dear old Bull, I think he did.

'No miracle!' I assured my client when we met in the cells at the end of the day, and he was half smiling when he said, 'No.'

'The universe has recovered its balance. There is a perfectly clear, scientific explanation.'

'I suppose so,' he conceded.

'They can't work miracles, Duchess! You've got nothing to be afraid of.'

'Haven't I?' He still sounded doubtful.

'You can tell the jury the truth now.' There was a long silence and then I pressed him again. 'Tell it! You've got to tell it for the sake of –'

'For *your* sake?' There was no mistake about it, he was smiling now.

I shook my head. 'For the sake of a lot of lonely people,' I told him, 'who go out looking for miracles.'

Chapter Nineteen

In a way, cross-examination is the easiest part of the defending barrister's job. You have the sword, the red cape to swing in the hope of exciting blind and intemperate anger, and, unless you slip on a pile of horse shit and get gored to death, you may hope to be in some sort of control of the situation. When you call your own client to give evidence in his own defence, however, the matter is entirely different. Out there in the witness box he is, for all practical purposes, beyond your help. You can't lead him, or put words into his mouth. For the first time in a trial he must tell his own story and in his own way, and all you can do is guide him towards the main points at issue and then leave him to sink or swim on his own. Calling your own client in a murder case is always an extremely dodgy and nerve-wracking business: what made it more alarming in Simpson's case was that I really had no very clear idea of exactly what he was going to say.

After the formalities of getting his name and previous good character were over, I started where I first heard of the Notting Hill Gate Underground Murder, in the Sunshine State.

'Last summer I think you went on a holiday to Florida. Did you meet someone in the street handing out leaflets?'

Once he began to talk, Simpson was articulate, and the old dead look had left him. 'He seemed so clean and respectable. He was wearing a tie and a clean shirt. We started to talk. About loneliness and how to make friends. Oh, and then about all the meanness and cruelty in the world. He took me to meet *his* friends.'

'Where were they?'

'In a sort of farm. It was called the Sun Valley. They were all nice and ... cheerful. They sang a lot, and they seemed to work very hard. Later I met a man, he was dressed as a clergy-man. They called him the Master.'

'What did he tell you?'

'My Lord. How can this be relevant?' Moreton Colefax rose to object, and, wonder of wonders, the Bull, impressed by the quiet young clerk in the witness box, said, 'I think we must let Mr Simpson tell his story.'

'What did he tell you?' I repeated the question gratefully.

'He told me I must work for him, in their accounts depart-ment. He said that when the Children of Sun took over the government of the world, I should have some great post ... in world economics. I was going to be their Minister of Finance.'

'Did you believe him?'

'Yes, I'm afraid I did.' Simpson smiled, a small apology for a huge presumption.

'Did you start to work on the books?'

'Almost at once.'

'What did you find?'

'There were hopeless discrepancies.' Simpson looked pained. 'A great deal of money was coming in: the "friends and brothers" gave all their worldly goods. None of this money was accounted for. I'm afraid I came to the conclusion that the whole organization of the Children of Sun was a gigantic swindle.'

'Did you tell anyone that?'

'We weren't allowed close friends. They told us that would destroy our loyalty to the group,' Simpson explained. 'But there was a young American man I worked with. I told him one night. He said he'd have to go to the Master and denounce me as a traitor. That's when I decided to escape. There was a truck going out of the farm gate with vegetables. I hid in the back of it.'

'And then?'

'Then I went back to England on the next plane. I'd man-aged to keep the ticket.'

'Back to your work in the Inland Revenue?'

'Of course.'

'Were you afraid at all?'

'Yes, I was. I knew I had found out things in Florida that the Children of Sun wouldn't want to be known. I told myself that I was back in England, and that they'd have no way of finding me, but I often got the feeling that I was being watched when I left home. Once or twice I thought I was being followed, nothing definite you understand, just an uneasy feeling.'

'Yes, I understand. Mr Simpson, will you tell me your routine movements on Thursday evenings?'

'Well, I used to go to my evening class.'

'In advanced accountancy?'

'Yes. And on the way home I would buy my supper at the Delectable Drumstick in Notting Hill Gate and take the train on to Paddington.'

'Anyone who had been watching you over a long period would know that?'

'Yes, I suppose they would.'

'Did you think anyone was following you, or watching you, on that evening of Thursday March the 13th?'

'I had an uneasy feeling. Nothing definite. Not until the man spoke to me on the platform.'

'The man?'

'Mr ... Canter.'

'Just tell the jury about that, will you, in your own words.'

He was out on his own; but I had no fear for him. The jury were listening attentively, and he told them, quietly and clearly, how that Sun Child, Rory Canter, tried to kill him, and how he fought with an unexpected passion for life, and how the knife was turned on his attacker.

When he had finished, I said, 'Mr Simpson. Why didn't you tell this story to the police when you were arrested?'

'I thought the power of the Master had changed the blood on the letter. I thought it was a miracle.'

'How do you feel, now you know it *wasn't* a miracle?'

'In a way, disappointed.'

'No miracle,' I told the jury in my final speech. 'Perhaps we are a little disappointed also, members of the jury, to discover that this is just another case about human violence and human greed. Or perhaps it is a case in which, after all, the Powers of Darkness had their terrible part to play.'

I was holding the knife, as a prop for the jury's attention, but I didn't need it. The old darlings were all listening intently as I went on. 'Mr Simpson discovered the secrets of a fraud practised upon the gullible and the lonely. Mr Simpson was to be killed, and a faithful servant of the Master, a young fanatic who had been trained in war, named Rory Canter, a man who'd just presented his own large property to this bogus Messiah, was to be the agent of death. What happened? Canter no doubt followed Simpson that night, and waited for him on the platform of the underground station. He accosted him and pulled the knife. He started the attack. You've heard from my client how these two men fought for this knife ... on which were the fingerprints of both of them. You've heard how my client's hands were wounded in the struggle and his clothes cut and, finally, forcing Canter's arm away from him, the point of the knife entered his attacker's body between the third and fourth rib. It was a desperate fight, members of the jury, because Canter was a man more dangerous than any thief or sexual molester; he was a man who believed he had God on his side ...'

The day the trial ended happened to coincide with the visit by Claude Erskine-Brown and young Tristan, attended by the large and glum Miss Reykjavik, to the Erskine-Brown grandparents for the few days' holiday Miss Trant's husband was taking from his never-increasing legal practice. According to plan, Ken Cracknell and Phillida shared their long delayed hamburger together in the All American Bun Fight in Covent Garden, and, although the minced meat was plentiful, the buns huge and the salad crisp, although they drank powerful vodka martinis and pursued them with bottles of icy Löwenbräu, and although Miss Trant held Ken's hand between mouthfuls and her eyes were full of promise, he remained inexplicably glum and apparently much cast-down by the result.

Determined to cheer the handsome radical barrister, Miss Trant returned with him, not without some misgivings, to the 'community' near King's Cross. This proved to be a comfortable and elegant Victorian house in a pleasant square behind the Grays Inn Road, which young Cracknell shared with a group of friends whose 'communal living' didn't go beyond sharing the kitchen and occasional meetings to 'talk through' problems in the 'interface of domestic group relationships'. In this community Ken Cracknell was undoubtedly the leader: he it was who organized applications to the Rent Tribunal and composed the notices urging consideration for others in the communal loo.

Fortunately most of his cohabitees were out when Ken brought Miss Trant home. She passed the sitting-room door (half open to emit the sounds of a middle-aged female voice reading some play she had written to an invisible audience) with some trepidation, and she didn't relax until they were in Ken's comfortable and brightly furnished bedroom. He had thoughtfully removed the bedspread and turned back the sheets before he went to Court that morning. She looked at the bed, smiled and kissed him. Then, as he drew the curtains and adjusted the lighting effects she took off her jacket, hung it neatly on the back of a chair and started to undo her shirt.

'Happy?' she asked Ken Cracknell. For an answer he returned to kiss her. '*Are* you happy, Ken?'

'Well ...' She was taking off her shirt and he was offering her, apparently, every assistance. 'Happy about you being here.'

'You should be happy about everything. You had a marvellous win!'

'Did I?' Ken Cracknell paused discontentedly in the act of disrobing Miss Trant.

'Of course Rumpole did it. But I'm sure you were a terrific help.'

'Rumpole!' Ken appeared unexpectedly angry and his fingers stopped working at the clips and buttons. Miss Trant looked up at him in surprise. 'Yes,' he muttered. 'Blast the man! Rumpole pulled it off.'

'What's wrong with that?' Miss Trant looked up at him puzzled.

At which Ken Cracknell burst out with thoughts which he had had to keep to himself for too long. 'What's wrong with it?

Don't you see? It means he'll never go. He'll be round my neck forever! Swamping the desk with his papers and dropping ash like a bloody volcano. That's not why I got him the job!'

'Why? Why did you get him the job, Ken?' She was moving away from him, looking at him with sudden suspicion.

'Well ...' He seemed, as he looked at her, to have some doubt about answering, but she insisted.

'Why did you get Rumpole to lead you?'

'It ... it seemed a hopeless case, anyway.' He was almost apologetic, and his apology gave her the answer.

'You wanted him to lose!' Now she was working hard, doing up all the clips and buttons that Ken had so eagerly, if awkwardly, unloosed. 'You thought he'd vanish back into the sunset if he lost another case. That's why you did it, isn't it? *You wanted him to lose!* So you could have him out of your room!'

'Philly ...' Ken's protest was ineffective. She continued to button, with determination.

'Well, let me tell you something.' Her eyes were no longer soft, but shining with the power of her sudden eloquence. 'You're wrong. Wrong about Rumpole. He's the radical! You're not. You'll grow up to be a prosecutor, or a Circuit Judge! But Rumpole never will, because he says what he thinks, and because he doesn't give a damn what anybody thinks about him. And because he can win the cases you're afraid even to do on your own.'

'Philly! Don't talk to me like that. Don't I mean anything to you?' Ken Cracknell moved towards her, pleading.

She looked at him and said, almost with regret, 'Oh yes. You're a pretty face around Chambers. A little bit of fluff! A reasonably good spot of crumpet. But don't ever get the idea I'd risk a good husband, who knows how to cook, for *you*, Ken Cracknell!'

Christmas came with its usual alarming rapidity. The season of God's birth was celebrated by cards and bits of tinsel appearing in the screws' office in Brixton Prison, and Hilda Rumpole and Marigold Featherstone sang an elaborate version of 'Come All Ye Faithful' with the Bar Choral Society in the Temple Church, to which the faithful, in the shape of their husbands Guthrie and Horace, dutifully came. I prepared for the occasion by buying what Hilda told me later was her fortieth bottle of lavender water, and she got me the usual gift-wrapped box of small cigars. She posted off innumerable articles of knitwear to Florida in time for Christmas, against the eventual birth of the next generation of Rumpoles. (In due course a boy arrived who was given the name Sam. I laid down a dozen bottles of Pommeroy's best claret for Sam on the top of the bookshelves in Froxbury Mansions. From what I hear the infant, although of tender years, is argumentative by nature and may make something of a career at the Bar.) I sent Nick my old copy of *The Oxford Book of English Verse* (the Sir Arthur Quiller-Couch edition) suitably inscribed. I know the poems I like best in it by heart, and doubt if I shall add many more to my repertoire.

A week or so before Christmas, cases of drink arrived at our Chambers. Dianne helped Henry put up tinsel and paper streamers in Guthrie Featherstone's room. They hung mistletoe from the central light and promptly kissed under it. On the night of our Chambers party, our members arrived with their wives and girl-friends. Henry's wife, a tall schoolmistress, came and put an end to his philandering under the mistletoe. Mr and Mrs Erskine-Brown came together and that small smiling Celt, Owen Glendour-Owen, came with a grey-haired wife who might have been his twin and was also smiling broadly. Uncle Tom brought his sister, who suffered hot flushes after a couple of glasses of sherry. My old friend Judge George Frobisher left his Court to come to our jollification, and Ken Cracknell arrived late by motorbike. The room was crowded when Guthrie Featherstone started to clear his throat, bang his glass against the desk and give every sign of a Head of Chambers who is about to make a ceremonial address.

'Quiet, everyone!' called out Henry, our self-appointed Master of Ceremonies.

'Pray silence' – I added my voice, after I had given myself a generous refill of Château Fleet Street – 'for our learned Head of Chambers.'

'Thank you, Horace.' Guthrie smiled graciously in my direction and then he was off. 'Christmas has put gifts in several of our stockings this year. Horace Rumpole had a very good win in an interesting murder down at the Old Bailey.'

'Did that surprise anybody?' I asked the world at large.

'It surprised Ken,' said Mrs Phillida Erskine-Brown, née Trant. Ken Cracknell glowered at her, whereupon she raised her glass to her husband Claude and said, 'Happy Christmas, darling.'

'And Owen Glendour-Owen,' Featherstone continued with our roll of honour or list of legal triumphs, 'has been appointed by the Lord Chancellor to the Circuit Bench. Our loss is mid-Wales's gain!'

'That's splendid news!' I raised my glass to the small Celtic couple. 'Absolutely splendid!'

I had done nothing but good to 'Knock-for-Knock' Owen, although I meant to take care to avoid Welsh Crown Courts in the future. When the cries of 'Splendid!', 'Yes, of course', 'Well done, Owen' and 'Good show, Judge' had died away, I quickly pointed out the full consequences of the joyful news. 'Which leaves an empty space in my old room,' I said, and looked hard at Featherstone. After all, he had made a private promise, and I wanted it publicly confirmed.

'Yes. Well, we'll consider that, of course. At a Chambers meeting.' It was typical of Featherstone to seek to put off the final, fatal decision. I wasn't letting him get away with it.

'We'll consider it now,' I insisted.

'I'm sure it's a matter you'll want to discuss with your family, Horace.' Featherstone tried to sound conciliatory. 'No one wants to force you back from your retirement, just because we happen to have a gap in Chambers. I'm sure Hilda has views.'

'Views?' No doubt Hilda had, she had about most things, but I didn't think she would feel called upon to speak at what was rapidly becoming a Chambers meeting. I was wrong.

'Yes, as a matter of fact I have,' she said, in a profound and doom-laden voice.

'Mrs Rumpole. Hilda. All in good time.' Featherstone clearly didn't want my wife's views to mar the festivities, but she overruled him.

'Since we got back from our holiday in the States ...' Hilda began.

'Holiday? Did she say holiday?' Uncle Tom was puzzled. 'I thought they'd gone out to grass. For good.'

'With our son, who, as you may know, is now the youngest Professor of Applied Sociology in the history of his university.'

'Oh, I say. Awfully well done him!' Marigold Featherstone gave a half-hearted clap and Guthrie smiled tolerantly.

'Since Rumpole's been back in harness' – Hilda was now in full flow – 'he has, of course, had an enormous success in a most important murder trial, and I am quite convinced that his real love is Judge Bullingham.'

'Really, Hilda!' I didn't know what she'd come out with next, but she looked at me and appeared to be smiling. 'I'm joking, of course,' she said.

'Oh, yes of course.' I was glad to hear it.

'Frightfully funny!' said Marigold Featherstone, and brought her hands together again.

'Most amusing speaker, your wife.' Featherstone's smile was slightly less tolerant.

'And I'm more convinced than ever that my duty is here, at Rumpole's side,' Hilda went on. My heart sank, I must admit it.

'Are you sure?' I asked hopelessly, but it seemed she had come to a firm decision.

'So I shall stay in England,' she said, 'to look after Rumpole.' She Who Must Be Obeyed had spoken and she only had one sentence to add. 'And we are *so* glad to be back in this happy family of Chambers.'

I thought the smiles were a little forced, and Ken Cracknell wasn't smiling at all. Only Mrs Erskine-Brown, our Portia, raised her glass to me, and I thought I noticed a tremor of one eyelid, as though she were about to wink.

'How long will you be staying this time, Rumpole?' Uncle Tom asked, and as I felt an old legal anecdote coming over me, I gave him his answer.

'How long?' I said. 'Who knows how long? I well remember that terrible old Lord Chief when I was first at the Bar. He gave an 86-year-old man fifteen years for persistent theft. At

Bodmin Assizes. "But my Lord," the old man quavered, "I shall never *do* fifteen years." "Well then, my man," the Lord Chief encouraged him, "you must do as much of it as you can." '

I looked round the room at them all. There was a sudden, rather chill silence. And no one laughed.

'That's all I can say,' I told them. 'I shall do as much of it as I can. And a very happy Christmas to you all.'